SUMMER CAMP FOR SLASHER VICTIMS

Edited by Danielle Yeager from Hack & Slash Editing
Cover Art by MiblArt
Paperback ISBN: 979-8-9903954-0-4

Hardcover ISBN: 979-8-9903954-2-8

eBook ISBN: 979-8-9903954-1-1

For Bean

"Absolutely not. I've seen enough corpses in
my life. I'll die before I see another one."

Content Warning

I start all of my books with a very general content warning. My books may contain graphic descriptions of death, gore, nudity, sexual situations, and plenty of other potentially offensive situations. To keep from spoiling the contents of *this* book, I won't guarantee that everything listed above will be inside, but it might. If any of this might make you uncomfortable, or if you don't want your child reading a story containing these contents, then this might not be the book for you or them. Otherwise, enjoy the story.

Prologue

Casey's headlights cut through the dense fog, casting an ethereal glow on the winding mountainside road leading to Camp Safe Woods. The mist hung heavy in the air, obscuring her view, as if she were driving through a mystical realm. The scent of damp earth and pine trees wafted through her car's vents, filling her lungs with the freshness of the wilderness. Excitement and nervousness intertwined within her, knowing that this would be her first job as a counselor at the camp she had cherished since her teenage years. The familiar faces of her camp friends, who would also join her, brought comfort amidst the jitters.

The thick fog enveloped her vision, reducing visibility to a mere twenty feet ahead. Each twist and turn along the treacherous mountain road only heightened her anxiety. Fearing the unknown dangers lurking, her mind raced with troubling thoughts. *What if a deer darts across my path? What if a reckless driver attempts to overtake in my lane? What if I miss my turn and careen off the cliff's edge?*

Despite the speed limit being fifty miles per hour, she dared not exceed thirty for her own safety. Tightly gripping the steering wheel, she leaned forward in her seat, straining to catch any glimpse of the road. Yet, an underlying unease persisted. Her father's warning echoed in her mind, urging her to delay the journey until the next day. However, the prospect of waking up early deterred her, and Mitch, the camp owner, had assured her she could sleep at the camp if she arrived early.

Her gaze fixated on the vibrant, dotted yellow line dividing the two lanes. A sudden yelp escaped her lips as she cruised past a weathered silver sedan, its paint oxidized, seemingly abandoned on the desolate roadside. The lack of a substantial shoulder made her heart race with concern, fearing a collision, but she narrowly avoided it—the distance between her vehicle and the sedan being just a few feet. She watched as it vanished in her rearview mirror, behind the fog and her car's exhaust.

As "Bark at the Moon" by Ozzy Osbourne blared through her car speakers, she couldn't help but find it amusing that the song played as she gazed at the dimly lit moon above, wishing it would provide more light for her drive. The thought of barking at the moon bounced in her head like Ozzy's vocals bounced around her car. Annoyed by the noise, she turned down the volume, hoping it would improve her focus and visibility.

This song was just one of many on this mix CD of '80s rock and metal, a compilation gifted to her by Max, her summer camp boyfriend. Max had started this tradition of making her a personalized CD every summer since they first attended camp together. It was a sweet gesture initially, as if he wanted her to carry a part of him back home. However, now she found it more bothersome than endearing. The songs on the CD were never her taste; she preferred more modern-day pop radio hits. Not only that, but Max would bombard her with questions about the music the following year, desperately seeking her approval.

"Which song did you like the most?" Or "What did you think of that mind-blowing guitar solo?" Or "Weren't his vocals on that track just life-changing?" Over the past couple of years, listening to the CDs had become a chore, something she saved for the car ride to camp. It was a task she endured just to be able to answer a few of Max's inquiries without hurting his feelings.

Sometimes she wanted to counter-interrogate him with questions like, "Why don't you listen to music released in this decade?" And "Who still burns CDs?" And "Why can't you just send me a Spotify link?" She wasn't even sure why or how they'd started either. Be it to make them both look more popular, or because they actually enjoyed each other's company at one point, or just because they needed the emotional support to withstand the time spent at a camp like this. But by now, she was ready to move on.

She figured since they were both adults now, she would spend just one final summer with him. On the last day, she planned to inform him she would be moving out of state for college and that it would be best if they went their separate ways. But before doing so, she was finally going to let him sleep with her. After years of enduring her, supporting her, and respecting her choice to wait, she believed he deserved it. It seemed like the perfect farewell gift

.

After a good half hour of driving up and over the mountain, the fog had cleared. But as one problem ended, another began. There was a loud *pop*, indicating she had hit something on the road. She hoped it was just plastic trash, but when the warning light on her dash showed low air pressure in her rear driver's side tire, she knew it was a problem. She noticed a green sign for a gas station at the next exit and decided to take it. After the exit, she made a right turn and headed down the long road that seemed to stretch endlessly into darkness.

The gas station looked less than inviting as all the lights were off, aside from the one advertising their prices of fuel, but even that seemed off: $3.42 for unleaded was significantly cheaper than anything she had seen in California in the year she had been driving. It was obvious this place was out of business, and it had been for a while. Still, she pulled up to the air pump to the right of the building and parked. She stepped out of her car, an Audi A5 Coupe her dad bought for her eighteenth birthday. Immediately, she heard the hissing from the back of the car, which confirmed her fear as she approached the flattening tire and saw the piece of scrap metal sticking out of it.

"Fuck," she muttered, her misty breath visible in the cold. She walked back to her car, grabbed her phone from the stand suctioned to her windshield, and looked at her GPS. She still had twenty-three miles to reach the camp. She looked at the air pump—clueless about how to even use it—then looked at her tire deflating lower to the ground with each passing second and decided it wouldn't help her anyway.

Thank God for roadside assistance.

She scrolled through the apps on her phone until she found the one her father installed for her insurance company and opened it. After waiting a few seconds, a cute picture of a dinosaur in the desert appeared on her screen, which denoted her lack of internet connection. She glanced at the top of her phone and saw the empty logo where the service bars would've been.

"Seriously?"

She noted the time on her phone: 11:36 p.m. Her dad would be long asleep by now, but she didn't really have a choice. She opened her contacts and found his name beside a picture of him asleep in his rocking chair with a newspaper covering his face. She pressed the <**CALL**> button, brushed her hair behind her ear, and raised the phone to it. It remained silent until it beeped once, indicating the call didn't go through. She looked at her phone, confused, and once again saw that she didn't have any service.

Really?

She steered her attention to the gas station and thought, *Why not?* Upon reaching the sliding glass doors, her assumption of the gas station being abandoned was confirmed—the doors didn't part open for her and all the lights were off except a single glow from an ice cream freezer. Still, she looked through the glass and knocked, hoping someone might still be inside. She gave up once she noticed how badly her breath fogged the window, then went back to her Audi. Once inside, she started the car again and turned on the heater. "No One Like You" by the Scorpions played—the only song on Max's CD she recognized and just another in a noticeable uptick of romantic songs on this year's playlist. More reason for her to feel worse about breaking things off with him.

She leaned back against the headrest, thinking of what else she could do to get out of this predicament, until she settled on her only real options: driving on the flat tire to camp, potentially destroying the Audi, or sleeping in her car until morning when people would be driving on this road, then flagging someone down to help her with getting the car towed.

She was tired enough, as she was already dozing off, so she settled on the latter option. Until she saw headlights illuminating her interior from behind. They glared brightly through the rear windshield, fogged from breathing in the cold interior, so she couldn't see who it was. She rubbed her eyes, turned off the car, and stepped out. "Hello?" she called as she closed her driver's side door and stepped toward the car. It was the silver sedan she had passed earlier.

Maybe they pulled over to pee.

"Thank you for stopping, I sort of have a flat—" She approached the car, peeked through the open window, and didn't finish her sentence once she saw that no one was inside. Confused, she looked around the sedan, then her own vehicle. With no sign of the car's owner, she turned her attention to the vacant gas station.

Did they get out of their car? I didn't fall asleep, did I?

"The gas station's closed!" she yelled, running to the building, expecting whoever had pulled over to hear her, but no one was there.

Maybe they work here.

Casey approached the sliding glass doors and half-expected them to work this time. When they didn't, she looked up at the motion detector above displaying a small red dot that looked back at her. Hoping it would see her and prompt the doors to open, she waved her hands, as if her movements from walking to the door would not be detectable in the dark. Still, no luck. Fed up, she dropped her hands and they slapped against her thighs. She looked back at the two cars parked one behind the other and thought she saw the shadow of a person walking toward her Audi.

"Hello!" She raised her head, trying to get a better view, and started a fast-paced walk back to the cars. "Sorry, I didn't see you before. I thought you went to the gas station." She stepped around the passenger side of her car, realized that she was still alone, then stepped back to the driver's side.

Are my eyes playing tricks on me? I could've sworn I saw someone.

She began to worry. Regardless of whether the owner of the sedan was trying to help her, she could not think of a justifiable reason for them to be acting so creepy. She thought of getting in her car and ditching the scene, but she looked at her flat tire, the rim now resting on the ground, and knew she couldn't outrun this person should they decide to chase her.

"Okay, just breathe and think, Casey," she told herself. She pulled her phone out of her pocket and checked the service, still none, and then the time: 12:12 a.m. "I'm gonna call the cops!" she yelled, bluffing. She waited, listening for the person to announce themself. They didn't.

She rushed into her car, locked the doors, and started it. She decided she would wait inside, and if this person wanted to help, they would come to the door and offer. If their behavior set off any red flags, she would immediately drive away. If someone was going to attack her, she wouldn't just sit idly and let it happen. All of her years at camp prepared her for times like this.

Camp Safe Woods isn't like any other summer camp. The owner designed this one with victims of serious trauma and significant loss in mind, organizing activities that teach kids suffering from PTSD how to feel safe and live a life where they don't feel the constant need to watch their back all the time. While any parent can send their kid there to teach them how to be more independent, they prioritize applications from kids who survived tragic events. For example, Casey.

She grew up in a small town within fifty miles of San Francisco. She had a hard time referring to her town as small, considering the millions of people that lived in California, but compared to other towns around hers, it was—or at least, it felt like it. Perhaps it was because she lived in a suburban neighborhood where the residents were extra friendly with each other that she felt like everybody knew everybody. The town was so small, in fact, that most of the kids who attended her high school were actually from out of town and had wealthy parents who were often busy and away on business trips, providing the perfect settings for enormous house parties. This list of parents included Casey's.

She was only thirteen, one year away from high school, yet Casey still found her way into these parties—primarily because her older sister, Courtney, would often throw them at their home. The only problem for her was that everyone there knew she was much younger and as Casey would say, "Not invited" to the parties. So they would keep her away from the alcohol, and all the kids, especially the boys, would avoid her like the plague. She spent most of her time during parties in her room, occasionally seeing action when two drunk teenagers would bust through the door, making out and looking for a place to release their teenage frustrations. She would simply shoo them away and go back to whatever she was doing: reading magazines, scrolling through Instagram, wishing she was old enough, e tc.

Her entire outlook on parties changed once the deaths started. That year, ruthless killings plagued her town, primarily targeting people in her sister's group of friends. It started with loose acquaintances and quick stabbings, but the violence escalated—organs spilled, a partial decapitation, even a hanging— and moved closer to Courtney. It scared Casey, not just because she worried for her own safety, but because she never knew if her parents would get the call that Courtney was the victim.

Her parents didn't seem as worried, though, as her dad still had a business trip to go on, and her mother had used the opportunity to have an affair—taking it to a hotel room and making up some story about needing to visit an old friend of hers who was hospitalized from a car accident to avoid the kids finding out. And Courtney wasn't too worried, either, because she still threw a party. She wouldn't live long enough to regret that decision.

Casey was lucky to miss most of the party as she locked herself in her room this time—a habit she developed, thanks to all the prior murders. Only during a break in a song playing through her computer speakers did she leave her room long enough to hear the screams. She stepped outside and saw that there were no more party guests. She spied bloody hand trails and splatter along the walls, overturned furniture, abandoned Solo cups spilled onto their carpet, and her sister sitting on top of the masked killer lying on his back atop bent metal and glass shards where their coffee table used to be.

Courtney unmasked the disguised murderer: her longtime boyfriend, Dennis, who responded by knifing her in the gut. At that moment, Casey noticed that her sister's stomach had already suffered multiple puncture wounds, and Dennis seemed to relish the moment as he repeatedly stabbed her. Blood spilled from her mouth onto her boyfriend's face and he laughed maniacally.

Casey screamed.

Dennis turned and saw her sitting on the stairs. He threw the now lifeless Courtney off of him, and Casey watched her sister's body hit the floor like a sack of potatoes before she ran. Dennis's footsteps stomped behind her. She didn't have a way to make it downstairs without passing him, so she had to go through her bedroom window and jump to the ground below, breaking a bone in her right foot that she would have to get surgically fixed later—another terrifying experience—but she maintained enough adrenaline to continue running until she caught up to the police vehicles racing to the scene.

She was lucky that one officer saw she was in danger. And she was lucky that her sister's blood on Dennis's face and the knife in his hand were enough to get that cop to pull the gun out of his holster and put a bullet in his head. She was unlucky, however, because when her mother returned home that night and saw her daughter's corpse on her living room floor, she overflowed with guilt—an emotion she was already wrestling with after her devious night of adultery—and ended her own life there, right beside her daughter. But not before going to the kitchen, finding pen and paper, and writing one last message to her husband detailing how her actions that night brought this divine judgment upon their daughter.

So just like that, Casey's life had flipped upside down, and everything she had ever known was gone. Their house became immortalized as a place that future documentaries and books would forever remember. She no longer trusted people, as she thought Dennis was once trustworthy, and feared doing anything, knowing that anyone could do something so horrifying. Her father came across the brochure for Camp Safe Woods when he was searching for a way to help his daughter properly cope with the loss, and it was perfect for him because he needed the alone time to cope. He knew he couldn't parent Casey the way he needed to, not after what happened, so he sent her off to camp, and surprisingly, she thought it worked. It took some time, but she no longer felt the same fears she did before, and she was ready to move on and experience life as an independent adult woman.

She heard a guitar solo playing quietly through her speakers, but it was too much noise for her when she felt the need to focus on what was going on outside, so she pressed the <**VOLUME**> button and turned it off. She yawned and rubbed her eyes. When she opened them, she looked out her door's window, then to the passenger side, then to the rearview mirror, and that was when she saw the figure—black hoodie, Camp Safe Woods baseball cap pulled low, sunglasses, camouflage bandana covering the rest of their face. Sitting in her back seat.

Before she could scream, a hand covered her mouth and held her against the headrest. The steering wheel constrained her as she tried to stand. She threw pathetic punches backward, connecting once and grazing them the second time, but it wasn't enough. They were strong.

She felt a warm liquid ooze on her stomach, looked down at the assailant's fingers, and saw the knife gripped by hiking gloves as they pulled it out of her. Then she watched them thrust it back in.

Is this what Courtney felt that night?

For the first time in years, Casey feared for her life like she always did in high school, yet this time was slightly different. Her hope had completely vanished. She coughed and watched the blood pour out between her attacker's fingers. Struggling to find air, she felt herself choking when she inhaled. She looked in the rearview mirror, hoping to identify who was stabbing her, but all she saw was the emotionless embodiment of her worst fears, as her blood splattered on the mirror and her vision blurred to the point that she could no longer see anything.

Chapter 1

Annie noticed the gas station sign at the upcoming exit and glanced at her fuel gauge. Not only was it nearly empty, but the low fuel light was glowing. She usually disregarded this warning back home, as she knew she could go at least another thirty miles before refueling. However, she hadn't come across a gas station in quite some time and worried there might not be another chance to fill up.

"Should I pull off here for gas?" she asked her grandfather, Mitch. "I'm running pretty low."

"No, that place is no good. They're abandoned. I know there's a cheap place closer to camp that's actually open," he said.

Annie never had a close relationship with her grandfather. Following his divorce from her grandmother, Alyssa, he distanced himself from the family, and she knew he took it hard. He dedicated himself to work until he had enough money saved to buy some forested land and establish Camp Safe Woods. From then on, he devoted all his time to the camp and studying ways to help patients who had experienced similar traumas to the one he and Alyssa had endured in their youth, then applying those methods at his camp.

That's why Annie's interest was piqued when on her eighteenth birthday, Mitch invited her to work as a counselor this summer. Without hesitation, she said yes. However, both her grandmother and her mom, Lauren, had concerns about the safety at the camp. To address their worries, Mitch arranged for them to visit the camp, take a tour, then drive him to Lauren's house, where Annie lived, so they could embark on the road trip together.

"Are you sure? My light came on already, and it looks like there's a car there."

"Yeah, we'll be fine. We are getting close to camp, and you won't need your car over the summer, so I'll just fill your tank before you leave to head home."

"You'd do that?"

"Why not? It's the least I could do." Mitch leaned into the back seat and pulled two pieces of licorice out of the giant tub they bought at the store before they left Annie's hometown. "Do you want one?"

"I'll be okay. Those things hurt my teeth."

"Suit yourself." Mitch put both pieces of licorice into his mouth, bit down, and tugged at them until they tore and his head recoiled against the headrest. He must've noticed Annie looking back and forth between the road and the fuel gauge when he said, "Look, if we run out of gas before we get there, I'll just push it the rest of the way."

She looked down at where his left leg was supposed to be, missing from the hip due to the aforementioned tragedy his grandparents experienced—an animal attacked their campsite, injured her grandfather, and killed several of their friends. Alyssa strictly forbade talking about this event, but Mitch was very vocal about it, insisting it was none other than Bigfoot that attacked them. If not for his missing leg and the questionable footage they got of the attack, Annie wouldn't have believed it ever happened.

She imagined him in his wheelchair, pushing the car up the road. Out of respect, she patiently waited for him to laugh first, as if his laughter gave her the go-ahead, and then joined in. They continued along the road for another ten minutes, and Annie noticed the route was now sur-rounded by trees. Growing up in California, she always knew that forests were nearby, but her mom never took her to see them in person because of what had happened to her grandparents. The trees were absolutely breathtaking. They stood tall, with triangular tops that reminded her of children's drawings of a house's rooftop. She had seen trees like these not only on TV and in internet photos but also back in high school, when she and her friends had secretly watched the footage of her grandparents' alleged encounter with Bigfoot that had been leaked online.

She admired the trees alongside Mitch as they watched them through the windshield. He looked serious and almost sad—a new look to Annie, who always saw him as an aloof bundle of comedic joy. She wondered if looking at the trees brought him back to those nights he spent suffering in the woods with his friends. She thought such a thing was obvious, but that only made her question why—if being here brought on such negative emotions for him—would he even start up a camp like this to begin with?

"So, what should I really expect while I'm working here?" Annie asked, snapping Mitch out of his trance. "You never gave me too many details about the job."

"Oh right." Mitch sniffled and sat up straight in his seat. "I mean, I wish I could say it was a simple gig. As a camp counselor, you have a lot of responsibilities. You need to watch the campers and make sure they aren't doing things they shouldn't. You're also going to help set up and supervise camp activities."

"Activities?"

"Yeah, there will be all kinds of things for the campers to do this summer. Things like painting, swimming, cooking lessons, archery—"

"Archery? Really?"

"Yep."

"How old are these kids? Can't archery be dangerous?"

"That's the whole point of this camp. Teaching these kids that even though the world is a dangerous place, we don't have to be scared to live in it. Archery is a fun activity for these kids, and it's a nice little self-defense lesson too."

"When I think of self-defense tactics, archery is pretty close to the bottom of the list." Annie laughed. "I think a gun makes more sense."

"While I agree, it would be a lot more difficult to convince these parents to let their kids use guns. And not just the parents, the government too. We'd get shut down so fast." Mitch slouched. "Besides, I wished I had a bow and arrow when Bigfoot came at me." He smiled, and Annie knew he was making a joke, but she didn't feel comfortable laughing with him. "Like I said, though, the job is super easy. We have a list of things that need to be done every day, like cleaning up, doing dishes, washing laundry, and making sure the kids are asleep by their bedtime. And we have a schedule of what activities will happen and when. If you have questions, just ask Nick."

"Nick?"

"Yeah, he's our head counselor. He has basically the same job as you, but he will play more of a lead role. He's been a camper here for years, and as soon as he was too old to attend, I promised him that job. Sweet kid, hard worker, but a little odd."

"Oh, how do you mean?"

"You know how Camp Safe Woods is a place for kids that have gone through trauma?"

Annie nodded.

"Well, Nick never did. His mom sent him to camp one year because she misread the brochure and thought it was more about teaching basic life skills. While she wasn't entirely wrong, she missed the part that mentioned PTSD. But Nick enjoyed camp so much that he kept coming back, even when he might've felt out of place among all those other kids. But he's grown into a fine young man over the years, and I'd like to think we helped with that. I'm excited to have him working for us. That's the thing you'll get to know about most people you meet on this job, counselors and campers alike—they all have their quirks, but they've been through some tough things."

"What can you tell me about the kids that come here? What can I expect?"

"It's really hard to say. Some of them—at least, the older ones—you couldn't even tell that they'd faced the horrid things they'd gone through. They've been coping for a while now and are learning how to act around others. And then you have those who have gone through things more recently. It is really hard to read those kids. Some of them are quiet, some are angry, and some are just plain mean. Honestly, I wouldn't worry too much about it. Just do your best to make sure the kids are nice to each other, remind them they've all gone through similar things, and when they want to talk to you about their problems, just listen to them. You will hear some awful, awful stories, and all you need to do is listen. The kids just want to be heard, and they need people to know what they've gone through without feeling like they're alone."

"Wow, it sounds like a lot to handle," Annie said.

"You'll get used to it." Mitch looked at the road ahead of them and pointed. "Oh, turn right here."

Annie made a turn and kept going along the narrow road until they reached another left turn. A large wooden sign hanging from a post marked the spot. The sign prominently displayed *CAMP SAFE WOODS*, but someone had defaced it with a red *X* that crossed out *SAFE* and replaced it with *DEAD*.

"Camp Dead Woods?" Annie asked.

"Yeah, some assholes do that every year. It's a nickname we've earned, given the tragic backstories of the campers who attend." Mitch sighed.

"That's awful."

"It's not so bad. The campers are mostly used to it, and some of them even use the nickname as a joke. But I had your grandmother paint a replacement sign for me, and she even added a pretty little painting of the camp's lake beneath the title."

"Really? That's so sweet. She loves to paint."

"I know she does. I miss painting with her."

"You guys just need to get back together already! I don't understand what's going on with you two. You obviously care about each other."

"Of course we do, and if it were up to me, we'd reunite in a heartbeat. Hell, we never would've divorced. But things aren't that simple, unfortunately." Mitch didn't look excited to be talking about this. He pointed just off the road to a couple of cars in a large dirt area. "You see those cars? That's where we park."

Annie parked the car and helped Mitch into his wheelchair. She grabbed her bags from the trunk of the car and handed her grandfather his things.

She followed Mitch as they walked through the parking lot and up a small path. Soon, she caught her first glimpse of the campsite. On either side of the road stood two impressively large log cabins. She hadn't been sure of their size, but Mitch had mentioned that each cabin could accommodate around ten campers, and now it all made sense.

In front of them stood a much larger building, also made of logs, proudly displaying an American flag hanging from a pole opposite the chimney. In front of the building was a spacious open area with log benches surrounding a massive stone firepit. Encircling the structure and common area were numerous tables with attached benches, reminiscent of the cafeteria tables Annie had eaten at during her high school days.

Outside the building, a young man and woman were busy hanging up an enormous banner that cheerfully proclaimed *WELCOME CAMPERS!* The man stood on a ladder, confidently nailing the banner onto the wooden structure, while the woman effortlessly supported the ladder with just one hand—helping but not helping.

The man wore a white tank top with khaki cargo shorts and work boots, and the girl wore a white crop top with black sleeves and cuffed denim shorts—as if they weren't already showing enough skin. Both of their shirts were decorated with a vibrant Camp Safe Woods logo.

"Vera! George! Come meet my granddaughter," Mitch yelled across the way.

They both turned their heads, causing George to lose his balance. The ladder wobbled back and forth as Vera scrambled to grab hold and help balance it. George leaped off the ladder, landing on Vera just as it fell to its side and crashed into the building's wall. Mitch immediately started wheeling toward them, and Annie ran ahead of him to offer assistance. George grunted as he stretched out his sweaty hand toward Annie. She tightly gripped it, causing him to accidentally push his other hand off Vera's wrist in an attempt to regain his balance.

"Ow!" she yelled.

"Shit, I'm sorry." Once he got up, he offered his hand to Vera, but she slapped it away and stood up herself. Annie noticed more sweat reflecting off his shoulders. Not that hot out this morning, so she knew he must've been working for a while today. That, or the fall made him sweat.

"You better not have torn a hole in any of my clothes!" Vera wiped the dirt off the back of her thighs and shook her head, examining her top.

"Are you guys okay?" Mitch asked when he caught up to them.

"Yeah, we'll be fine," George said.

"Speak for yourself." Vera lifted each leg and arm, inspecting them with great detail. She was fine. "I'm sure I'll feel it later."

"So, you said this was your granddaughter?" George asked, bringing his attention to Annie.

"I did. She's gonna be a counselor with you guys this year."

"My name's George." He held his hand out.

"I'm Annie." She shook it.

"It's nice to meet you. I'm Vera."

"Great, now that you're all acquainted, where are the others?" Mitch asked.

"Jenna and Max are checking out the lake. Neil is resting in the cafeteria. Casey hasn't shown up yet. Max keeps complaining that she isn't answering her pho—" George said before Mitch interrupted.

"What about Nick?"

"Nick's working with us? Don't you think he should've moved on by now?" George asked.

"Let's try to be welcoming to everyone, please. And that includes the counselors. I'll assume that he just hasn't made it yet," Mitch said.

Annie spotted two more individuals approaching them from behind a cabin deeper into the camp. One was a Hispanic girl with her dark black hair neatly tied back in a ponytail. She was wearing shorts overalls with one suspender casually hanging off her shoulder and a black one-piece swimsuit underneath. The other person was a preppy-looking Caucasian male sporting a dark blond comb-over. He was dressed in tight jeans and a light blue polo shirt.

"Oh, who's this?" the girl yelled and ran to them.

"This is Annie, my granddaughter," Mitch explained.

"Granddaughter? I didn't know you could reproduce," the new guy joked.

"It's nice to meet you both." Annie laughed.

"Nice to meet you too! I'm Jenna. Please tell me you're working with us!" She jumped with excitement.

"I am." Annie smiled, a tad overwhelmed by Jenna's energy.

"Yay!" Jenna yelled and hugged her.

"The guy waved awkwardly and put his hands in his pockets. "My name's Max." Annie made a mental note that he was the socially awkward type.

"God, you all are so loud," a voice called from the large building behind Vera. Annie turned and saw a man standing in the doorway. To say he was out of shape would be putting it lightly—he was rotund. With his greasy hair and undersized shirt, Annie chose to avoid an introduction.

That must be Neil, and this building must be the cafeteria, she gathered from when George mentioned the counselors who had arrived.

"How am I supposed to get any sleep with you guys making so much noise?" Neil asked.

"You're not supposed to be sleeping, you're supposed to be working," Vera said.

"I'm helping the cafeteria lady get set up. Duh. I'm talking about every night I'm forced to spend with you guys this summer."

"First off, 'the cafeteria lady' has a name, and it's Betty. And second, you can sleep when you're dead. Third, nobody is forcing you to be here," Vera said.

"Okay, calm down, guys. The campers haven't even arrived yet. Let's leave the pointless bickering to them," Mitch said.

Vera stuck her tongue out at Neil.

"I see the party started without me," a man said from behind them.

There are more people? Annie thought to herself. She turned and her eyes met a tall, lanky guy with a crew cut so blonde it seemed to shimmer in the sunlight, a stark contrast to Max's darker hair. His bright red shorts clung to his thighs, the fabric resting just above his knees. A white shirt decorated with the vibrant logo of Camp Safe Woods covered his torso. With his left hand, he dragged a heavy suitcase behind him. Over his other shoulder, he carried a duffle bag.

Following closely behind him was a goth-looking girl, her presence almost scary. Her jet-black '80s hairdo framed her face, the strands curled down to her shoulders. The scent of her well-worn leather jacket mingled with the faint aroma of cigarette smoke. Clad in tight-fitting skinny jeans that hugged her slender frame, her every step screamed confidence and rebellion. She pulled a suitcase; the wheels rolled smoothly, while a small backpack dangled from the handle, swaying with each movement.

"Nick!" Mitch threw his hands in the air with excitement. "What took you so long?"

"I had to pick Jordan up from the bus stop," Nick said.

"You still aren't driving?" Vera asked.

"I have a car, but why would I bring it? It's not like we can use them at camp. Besides, do you know how expensive gas is in California?" Jordan asked.

"Ah, shit," Mitch said. Annie looked at him and he seemed confused, counting on his fingers.

"What is it?" Annie asked.

"I just remembered. I try to keep an even distribution of boy and girl counselors. That way, we can assign one of each to each cabin, and every camper can feel safe and have someone to talk to. I completely blanked when I saw

Jordan's name and assumed she was a boy. We might be a little uneven this year."

"I think you did it right. I count four of each here," Jenna said.

"Yeah, but Casey hasn't shown up yet," Max said. He sounded upset. "I still haven't heard from her either."

"Maybe she bailed?" Jordan offered.

"I wouldn't put it past her," Nick agreed.

"Is anyone else coming? When she gets here, we'll have an uneven number," Vera said.

"No, nobody else. We're supposed to have eight counselors, two to each cabin, and the head counselor, Nick, who is supposed to oversee everything," Mitch explained.

"I'm sure she'll get here, eventually. If she doesn't, I'll take her spot in watching over a cabin and still oversee everything else. It shouldn't be a problem. But,"—Nick dropped his duffle bag and dug out a drill—"we have work to do and the campers will start arriving in the morning. Let's make this place nice and clean before they get here."

"Okay, I'll leave you guys to it. I'm gonna see if Betty can run me around for a few errands. I'll be back by nightfall. And tonight, we are having our special counselors only campfire, so be prepared for that," Mitch said. All the counselors cheered. It sounded fun.

Chapter 2

After Annie left her bags in the cafeteria, she spent the afternoon completing different chores around the camp. Nick, who she believed didn't really like her, supervised her during these tasks. While he got along well with the other counselors, he appeared distant toward Annie, almost ignoring her. Whenever she had questions, he responded with seemingly annoyed answers. Despite this, Annie chose to overlook it and made an effort to be kind to him.

Her first unsupervised chore for the day was to check the stability of things around the campsite, like wiggling wooden boards on benches in the dining area and the pier at the lake to make sure everything was in place and a kid wouldn't fall through. Mitch didn't charge a lot of money for kids to be here and therefore made little profit. A lawsuit wasn't something the camp would likely survive.

The lake was large and pretty. She had imagined it would be a lake with a sandy beach, but this one had pebbles and trees close to the shoreline. After hours of walking around the campsite and testing the stability of all the benches while the sun rose to its peak and started beating down on her, she was tired and overheated, so she thought she could use a break.

Stepping onto the pier, she carefully walked toward its end, ensuring that each board was secure. Arriving at her destination, she took off her shoes, removed her socks, and placed them inside her shoes to prevent them from being carried away by the breeze into the water. Seating herself at the edge of the pier, she rolled up the legs of her jeans past her calves and gently dipped her feet into the water, submerging them up to her ankles. Initially, the coldness was a shock, but as she acclimated, it began to feel invigorating. Surprisingly, the water was crystal clear and icy to the touch. She playfully kicked and splashed, cooling her shins before finally reclining and shutting her eyes.

She felt tranquil, almost too much so. Worried about potentially being needed by other counselors or being caught slacking off by Nick while the rest of the team was busy, she was anxious about not being reachable in this setting. She already thought he didn't like her, and she didn't want to compound that, so she pulled her legs out of the water and stood on her left leg to kick the water off of her right, before pivoting to the other and repeating the process.

When she got back to camp, her next task was to work with Jenna and follow instructions Betty had written on a whiteboard in the kitchen before she left camp with Mitch. Jenna explained that one of their traditions is to greet the kids with a huge barbecue feast. Most of the kids are transported via a bus that collects them; they all arrive around the same time so the camp knows when to have the food ready. Betty liked to prepare for this the night before, and their instructions were to season the ground beef and shape it into hamburger patties.

Even though her mother was great at cooking, Annie never was. She didn't see the point. Whenever she tried to cook something, it either burned or stayed cold. On about three occasions, she'd even set things on fire. Early in her high school years, she gave up on the kitchen altogether and decided her mom's food would always be good enough. And when it was time for her to move out, she would find a man who knew what he was doing in the kitchen.

Sure, she wasn't cooking the burgers herself, but she still had no idea how to shape them, yet Jenna looked like a pro. Annie spent about five minutes trying to shape one ball of meat into a circle, and once she got the shape down, it looked like a mushy, unappetizing mess. She looked over to Jenna's side of the counter, and she already had four perfect patties laid out on the tray. Jenna must've felt her looking that way because she turned her head to Annie and noticed her soggy meat pile. She giggled.

"Do you need some help?" Jenna asked, but she was already approaching and reaching into Annie's bowl of meat.

"Please."

Jenna pulled out a handful of meat and rolled it into a perfect ball shape with her palms. "So you want the ball to be about this big." She placed it on the counter and turned around, opening a drawer from the counter behind them, and pulled out a steel utensil that Annie had never seen before. It was metal with a flat, circular base and a handle. "If you can't get the shape with your hands, use this." Jenna pressed the object onto the burger, and once she pulled away, the meat had settled into its perfect shape. Jenna handed the tool to Annie.

"Wow, thank you! And it doesn't even look like it's melting," Annie said.

"Yeah, they get mushy like that if they get too much body heat from your hands. The burger press just makes things faster and smoother."

"Do you have any tools that make it so I don't have to dig into this cold pile of meat?" Annie asked, reaching for the next ball of ground beef at her station.

Jenna laughed. "I don't, I'm sorry! But I have a lot of other tips and things I'll show you this summer. I was a counselor here for the first time last year, so I know how hard it can be. But I figured out all kinds of stuff to make this job easier."

"Well, I can't wait to hear them. I don't know the first thing about camping."

"Really? I thought you would, since you know ... Mitch is your grandfather and all."

"Believe it or not, Mitch isn't the biggest fan of camping," Annie said.

"Yeah, that's understandable. I mean, what he went through was just awful."

"Oh, he told you about that?" Annie was shocked. Mitch wasn't very private about the accident, but she wasn't sure if he actively told his employees, or anyone at the camp for that matter, about the accident.

"He tells everyone about it!" she exclaimed. "It's not like he keeps it a secret. I'd say he was even proud of it."

"Is that right?" This took Annie by surprise, considering how private her grandmother always was regarding the matter.

"He promises everyone that he will tell them his story of what happened at the end of every summer. As if it were an incentive. Don't get me wrong, I knew about what happened a long time ago, like, who hasn't watched the tapes yet? But he treats all of us like he has some big secret that he can't talk about until the campers are grown and ready to hear it, then he spills the beans during the final campfire of the summer."

"Oh! That's so crazy. I never would've that he'd treat it like that, considering how everyone in my family did their best to keep it away from me."

"It's a big thing. Almost like a rite of passage for us. Like, once we've all grown up and gotten over our issues, we finally get to hear about what happened to him. I remember being so excited when I heard it for the first time. And the story, even though I already knew what happened, was a great experience to hear coming straight from him. Your grandpa is ... he's a really good guy."

Annie smiled. Though she didn't have the closest relationship with Mitch, she always looked up to him. She was glad he could impact these kids in such a bright way despite what he'd gone through. "So ... you were a camper here, then?" Annie asked.

"Yeah. I'm just as fucked-up as everyone else you'll meet here."

"And this place ... did it help you?"

"More than you could ever understand. I used to be very timid. I had no friends, and I was afraid to leave my house—which wasn't a great characteristic for me to have because my house was where all my problems started. Everywhere I looked, all I saw was death. Yet, leaving wasn't an option for me. My parents basically had to drag me onto the bus to send me here. I cried the first few nights, but by the end of the summer, I didn't want to leave! I had never felt safer—at least, not since the killings. And trust me, home was the last place I wanted to go."

"Wow. I never would've guessed. I mean, timid is the last word I would use to describe you, and we've only just met."

"Exactly! I've made so many friends at this camp and my entire life has turned around in a way I never thought possible. I owe it all to your grandfather. He really made living a happy life possible for me."

Wow, Annie thought. She finished pressing down the patty she had been working on and noticed that she had already finished a dozen while they were talking. "Knowing him, he probably doesn't realize how big of an impact he's made on all of you guys. But I know that this place brings him a special joy, and I think you guys are helping him work through his problems just as much as he is helping all of you."

Jenna smiled.

"So, what was it?" Annie asked.

"What was what?"

"The thing that made your parents seek this camp? I heard you mention killings—"

"How dare you ask me about that!" Jenna interrupted.

Annie dropped the burger press as her stomach sank.

What was I thinking? That's so rude!

Jenna pointed at her, and her serious face transitioned into a smile. "I'm just fucking with you. But look at your face! You look like you just witnessed a slaughter of your own." She held the counter as she laughed with each word.

"You scared the shit out of me."

"I hope not! We don't wanna contaminate the burgers." She kept laughing.

Annie grabbed a nearby hand towel and playfully tossed it at her. "So there were no killings, then?"

"Oh, there were." Jenna picked up the towel from the floor, folded it, and placed it on the counter. "I've just learned to joke about it after all this time. It helps me cope. Why be sad when you can be happy, right?"

"I guess." Annie shrugged.

"It happened when I was a kid. A bunch of parents in my town went out to a costume party on Halloween night, leaving their kids at home with babysitters." She grabbed more meat and started rolling it in her palm before pressing it flat. "What they didn't know was that somebody escaped from the local psychiatric ward the night before. He found his way into our neighborhood looking for his childhood home, where rumors say he killed his family on Halloween night thirty years before."

"Oh my God!" Annie exclaimed, holding her mouth with her palm. She had forgotten her palm was covered in ground cow carcass until she felt the slimy texture caressing her cheek. She pulled her hand away and wiped her face with her inner elbow before pretending she didn't just do that, and hoping Jenna hadn't seen it happen.

"He started three doors down from mine ... at my friend Brian's house. He was watching scary movies in the living room while his poor babysitter was making popcorn in the microwave. They said he put the knife in just below her belly button and pulled it upward until it got caught on her sternum. They said she would've lived long enough to watch her blood spill onto the floor, where he ultimately let her body drop. If she was screaming, Brian couldn't hear it between the movie and the popcorn popping."

Annie kept quiet. She thought of what to say, but there were no words.

"He crossed the street, inconspicuous to those around him because people thought the blood on his outfit was part of a Halloween costume. When he got to my friend Rachel's house, the babysitter had already sent her to bed. She invited her boyfriend over, and they were getting it on in Rachel's parents' bedroom. According to rumors, someone cut her up first, and her boyfriend mistook her screams for an early climax. He died before he knew any better. One stab, straight into his head."

Annie wanted to laugh. The story seemed so outrageous, but Jenna's face moving in a gloomy direction reminded her that this was someone's life—something she knew she would have to remember for all the kids she would hear from this summer.

"Finally, he made it to my house, which just so happened to be his childhood home. My babysitter, Lauren, was his final victim."

Lauren! That's my mother's name, Annie thought.

"She was the nicest person ever. If I finished my homework early enough, she would let me stay up extra late and eat ice cream! She also took me out trick-or-treating, even when my parents gave her strict rules to keep me safe inside the house. To keep it a secret, we would eat all the candy together and stuff the wrappers in her purse, so she would take the evidence with her when she left the house. And she let me eat all the good candies while she ate all the ones I didn't like! She was a lot of fun. Unfortunately, we never got away with our little secret because someone murdered her before she could take the wrappers with her. My parents did eventually find out, but they couldn't bring themselves to punish me for it since they thought watching my babysitter get stabbed thirty-seven times was punishment enough."

"Wow, lucky you," Annie joked, happy that Jenna caught the sarcasm as they joined each other in a laugh.

"Right?" Jenna placed her last burger down. "Get ready for a bunch of stories like mine while you're here. This camp encourages the kids to talk out their problems because they need to understand that although their trauma isn't entirely normal, they aren't alone. I can only imagine how hard it will be for someone like you to hear about things like this when you haven't gone through it your-self." She turned on the sink and started scrubbing the muck from her hands.

"It can't be anywhere near as hard as what you guys went through. Besides, I grew up hearing these crazy Bigfoot stories from my grandparents."

"You think they're crazy?" Jenna dried her hands with the hand towel she put on the counter earlier and pointed at the burger in Annie's hands. "Oh! After that one, we should be good."

Annie gave her a red-stained thumbs-up. "I wouldn't say crazy, but I don't know that I believe the whole story."

"Yeah, I get that."

"How well did Nick handle it?" Annie put her last burger patty down.

"What do you mean?" Jenna stood in the open doorway, leaning on its frame and looking into the main dining area.

"You said it might be hard for me having not gone through something of my own … How was it for Nick? Mitch told me he only came to this camp on some sort of fluke." Annie washed her hands with warm water and dish soap from the industrial-sized bottle beside the faucet.

"Oh right! He …"—Jenna looked up at the ceiling, as if visualizing her thoughts until she spotted her answer—"I guess he handled it pretty well. Even though he was often teased, he kept coming back for years. And he must've liked this place enough to come and work here."

"He was teased?" Annie dried her hands with the same hand towel as Jenna.

"Yes. A lot. I think other campers were jealous that he hadn't gone through the same type of shit we have. And that was pretty much what they said when they had teased him, 'You don't belong here.'"

"Wow."

"Yeah, kids can be harsh. But you'll be fine." Jenna's eyes shifted outside as something caught her eye. "I think Mitch just got back, and it's going to turn dark soon. We should go help set up the campfire.

"Let's do it," Annie said.

Chapter 3

"First of all, I want to thank you guys for being here," Mitch said, as he wheeled his chair across the dirt to join them in the circle around the raging fire.

The counselors all sat atop the wooden log benches. Jenna had just told Annie that she was part of the group of campers tasked with making them a couple of years ago. The firepit was massive, constructed from cinder blocks stacked eighteen inches high, forming a circle with an eight-foot radius that contained a pile of wood the counselors found and placed in the center.

Mitch had a grocery bag in his lap from which he pulled out a bag of wooden skewers, took one, then passed the bag to Neil, who sat on the bench to his right by himself. "I know for most of you, this is your first job ever, and that's a big deal. Knowing what you kids have gone through and watching you grow into the adults that stand before me, I just want to say that I'm proud of you all. Sometimes it's hard to get out of bed in the morning and even harder to leave the house. But to accept a job and commit to it ... Not everyone can do that."

"Yeah, like Casey," Vera said.

"I'm sure she has a good reason for not showing up." Max took a skewer from the bag George gave him and passed it to Jenna.

"Probably to get away from you—"

"Ouch!" Annie yelped, interrupting Vera after she took the skewers from Jenna, reached into the bag, and a splinter entered her middle finger. She felt the group looking at her while she examined it, but the flames' inconsistent light wasn't enough to help her see the wound. She passed the bag to Jordan on her left.

"Max is right," Mitch said. "I'm sure she had a good reason. Even if it was just too much for her, that's a good reason. Think about it. I'm sure there was a point in time where each of you didn't want to come to this camp for a whole summer. Maybe this was her time. She's an adult now. She probably just moved on, and that's fine. Honestly, that's the whole point of this place."

Max repeated his concern voiced earlier, "I'm just worried about her. She isn't responding to any of my messages."

"If she really wants to move on, that includes you," Vera said, grabbing the skewers from Jordan.

Max gave her a dirty look.

"Why are you such a bitch?" Jordan asked.

Vera shrugged.

"Honestly, she probably knew you would try to convince her to come. And she is fully aware of our camp rule, which starts tonight," Mitch said, leaning forward and pointing to Nick, who just grabbed his skewer and set the bag down. The counselors, aside from Annie, nodded.

"That rule is real?" Vera moaned.

"I thought you guys just told us that as campers so we couldn't complain," George said.

"Nope, it's real," Nick said, picking up a plastic bag from the ground behind the wall of cinder blocks in front of him. He held the empty bag open in front of Vera.

"Wait, what's going on?" Annie asked.

"Nobody at camp can have their cell phone," Jenna said, pulling her phone from the pocket of her overalls. "That includes the counselors."

Annie was taken aback as she looked around and saw everyone else reaching for their phones. Vera, expressing her annoyance, rolled her eyes and dropped her phone into the bag. Nick approached Jordan, who nonchalantly dropped her phone in as well. Annie glanced at her grandfather, hoping he would confirm that it was all just a prank, but he simply nodded in agreement.

"You never told me I couldn't have my phone," Annie said to Mitch.

"You wouldn't have come."

"You don't know that."

"Well prove me wrong."

Annie sighed and took her phone from her too-small jeans pocket and placed it in the bag, careful not to let it fall too hard on another phone.

"We will lock the phones in a secret location that only Mitch, myself, and one additional counselor chosen randomly will be aware of," Nick rambled, as he continued collecting phones around the firepit. "Mitch only made two keys. Currently, I have them both and will give one to that randomly chosen counselor. This is only for an emergency case scenario. If you are selected, you have the responsibility to keep it hidden unless absolutely necessary. This goes for the counselors' phones and the campers' phones."

"But what if we need to make a phone call?" Annie asked. "You know, like, if something happens to one of the campers."

Nick took Neil's phone and closed the bag.

"As everyone who has already attended the camp knows, there is a single landline phone inside the cafeteria. It is bright red and will only make calls to nine-one-one," Nick explained.

"What about your phone? I didn't see you put yours away," Vera said, pointing at Nick.

"Oh right." He dug into his back pocket, pulled his phone out, and put it in the bag. He walked back to his seat, placed the bag on the ground, and sat down.

"But what if my mom calls to ask how I'm doing? She's gonna worry if I don't respond," Annie said.

"Your mom already knows the rule," Mitch said. He opened the bag in his lap and pulled out some marshmallows. He took one out for himself, placed it on his skewer, and passed the bag to Neil. "I told her before we left."

"Of course you did," Annie muttered under her breath, giving up.

"But what if Casey texts me back? What if she needs help?" Max asked, skewering his own marshmallow and passing the bag to his left.

"Then she should call the authorities." Nick reasoned.

"Now, for our first order of business: roasting marshmallows," Mitch said.

Max and Jenna clapped. Annie, George, and Vera sighed; Annie's more exaggerated than the rest, drawing attention from the other counselors.

"Sorry, I just hate marshmallows," Annie said.

"You hate marshmallows?" Nick asked.

"When you grow up related to someone who takes them as seriously as Mitch does, the magic fades away."

"Ignore her. You're all about to get a lesson from a professional," Mitch declared. He wheeled his chair closer to the firepit and leaned in, extending his skewered marshmallow out toward the flame. "First, you need to understand that this is something that takes time. Marshmallows are delicate, and you can't rush it."

Annie rolled her eyes.

As soon as Jordan passed the bag to Nick, she held hers directly in the flame. She pulled it out and watched the flame scorching at its tip.

"Otherwise, you'll ruin it. As Jordan was so generous to demonstrate," Mitch said.

"I prefer them this way." Jordan blew out the flame and spun her skewer to maintain the melting marshmallow's balance and keep it from falling. "Do we have any graham crackers?"

"Sure, here." Mitch rustled in the plastic bag and pulled out a box that he tossed to Jordan. "And take this too." Once she opened the crackers, pulled one out, and broke it in half, Mitch tossed her a chocolate bar.

"Thanks." She broke off some chocolate and placed it on the bottom half of her cracker. Then she squished the marshmallow with both halves and pulled it off the skewer.

Meanwhile, the other counselors all skewered their own marshmallows and began roasting while Mitch continued to rotate his.

"The trick is to keep it just outside the flame. Close enough to get the right amount of heat, but don't touch it or it will burn. When the flame moves, move with it," he said.

"How do we know when it's done?" Max asked.

"The marshmallow will be black," Jordan said as she took a bite from her s'more.

"Nope. That's just wrong. You're looking for a perfect golden brown color." Once I finish mine, I'll show you," Mitch said.

"Give him about twenty more minutes," Jenna joked, and the counselors laughed.

"You're laughing now, but wait until you see this thing. While we wait, let's move on to our next order of business." He snapped his fingers at Nick, who picked up a box from behind the firepit.

As he opened it, he retrieved several black, sealed bags that resembled the packaging used by online stores to ship clothing. The counselors, except for Annie, let out a collective groan. It was evident that they recognized the bags, making Annie feel left out. Nick made his way around the campfire, distributing a bag to each counselor. Each bag had a large piece of paper taped to the outside, bearing the name of the respective counselor. Finally, he placed the last remaining bag back into the box, which Annie assumed belonged to Casey.

"Do we have to wear this stuff?" Vera asked, ripping open her package.

"Have you ever seen a counselor without them?" George asked. "Besides, isn't the shirt you're wearing the same?"

"I put this on to show support for the camp. I thought it would be cute for a couple of days, but a full summer is ridiculous."

Annie cautiously opened the bag, revealing a shirt that matched the style worn by George, Vera, and Nick. Her shirt was white with red trim around the collar and sleeves, adorned with the Camp Safe Woods logo in the center. Assuming that they all received similar shirts during their time as campers, Annie placed her shirt on the bench. She then discovered three more identical shirts, along with a crop top and a long sleeve shirt, all featuring the same designs. Beneath the tops, she found three pairs of bright red booty shorts with the camp logo at the bottom of the left leg, as well as some white tube socks embellished with three red stripes at their tops.

"Really, Grandpa?" she asked, holding up the shorts.

"Cool, right? And they're free for all counselors. The campers have to pay for theirs," he said.

"These are way too short!" she protested, examining them closer.

"But they're really soft," Jenna said, pressing her pair to her cheek.

"That's nice and all, but my ass is gonna fall out of them. Aren't we gonna be looking after kids?"

"You'll be fine. Besides, it gets hot out here, so you'll be glad to have them," Vera said.

"If they make you uncomfortable, the shorts are optional. I expected you to have already packed sweatpants or other bottoms, but every day until the campers are put to bed, all counselors must wear the shirts. For camp spirit, you know?"

Annie exhaled.

"I don't see what the problem is. I like mine," George said, holding up a pair much longer than the girls' shorts. They were the same kind that Nick had been wearing all day.

"Let me get this straight. The guys get to wear regular shorts while the girls have to wear clothing that promotes their objectification throughout the day?" Jordan asked. She didn't seem the type to wear shorts, regardless. She carried herself strong with an edgy, tomboyish, rebellious, bad girl style.

"I ... uh—" Mitch fumbled over his words until Jordan cut him off.

"I'm only kidding. I've actually been looking for a pair like this," she said.

Mitch still appeared stunned. As if he could see the discriminatory lawsuit written out in front of him.

"Seriously, thank you," Jordan reassured him and stood up, holding the shorts to her legs, imagining how they would fit.

Mitch sighed and looked down at his marshmallow. He got so excited, he almost jumped out of his seat—if only he could. "Aha! Look at that!" He held his skewer high in the sky. The marshmallow at its peak was a dark brown and followed down to its base in a gradient that flowed into a gold and, finally, a white line at the bottom. "The perfect marshmallow. This is how they are supposed to be, Miss Jordan." He waved the skewer around, doing his best to give everyone a view of it.

Annie couldn't help but be impressed. She looked down at her own; it was still burning and cracking at the tip, and it was completely uneven in its cook. She looked around the group and they all looked either similar or worse—aside from Jenna, who almost had it, and Nick, who was less than a minute away from perfection.

Mitch sandwiched his golden brown glob between chocolate and crackers and sunk into his seat, staring into the crackling flames while he enjoyed consuming his treat.

"So we have one last official order of business we should discuss before we get too lost in this fire," Nick said. The counselors just looked at him, some of them giving up on their perfect marshmallow dreams and turning them into s'mores; Jordan burning hers and eating it straight, without the other ingredients. "We have to designate cabin leaders. Like we said before, we want a boy and a girl to be the leader of each cabin. Keep in mind that we will assign you to a particular cabin for the entire summer, as our campers rely on that kind of stability. We don't know how much anxiety we could cause if a kid gets attached to you and loses that sort of parental/older sibling figure."

"Your roles as cabin leaders are simple but important, Mitch added. Perhaps the most important task for you is to keep track of your campers. Learn their names, remember their faces, and make sure you know where they are at all times. If a kid goes missing ... Well, we wouldn't be able to call ourselves Camp Safe Woods anymore now, would we?" Mitch joked. He held his second marshmallow right outside the flame. The counselors observed him silently; the only noise between his sentences was the crackle of the flames. "You will also need to listen to your campers whenever they need someone to talk to. As you all know, a big part of this camp is learning to manage your problems—not avoid them. This means being able to talk about them openly and not being afraid of them. But that doesn't mean force the kids to talk about it. They will come to you when they're ready. That's our goal here. Getting them ready. And not just for talking about their problems, but getting them ready to go back into the real world, prepared to live a normal life without having to constantly watch their backs. Does everyone understand?"

Annie looked around the group and the counselors all responded the same. Each of them looked at Mitch and nodded.

Nick let out a sigh, stood from his seat, and said, "Okay, so there are two ways we could've done this: pull our names from a hat or just choose who we want to run our cabins with. I figured if we picked our partners, we would be more prone to goofing around instead of ensuring the campers' safety. So I've taken the initiative and already wrote the names of the boy counselors and put them in my hat." Nick pulled an upside-down snapback hat from behind the campfire; it was white with a red brim and a red Camp Safe Woods icon decorating the front. "I'll let each girl pick out a name, and they will partner up with the name they pull—no exceptions." Nick stepped behind Vera and held the hat over her left shoulder, beside her cheek.

She extended her right hand across her chest and reached into the hat, shuffled what Annie believed to be small pieces of paper, pulled one out, and unfolded it.

Nick must've seen what the paper said because he nodded and said, "You're with me." But Annie only saw the look of disappointment on Vera's face—spelled out with a long, exaggerated blink—as the realization set in.

Nick stepped close behind Jordan and held the hat beside her cheek, even closer. She turned her full torso around to reach into it, distancing herself ever so slightly from him. Annie was noticing things like this. The little tendencies that these people have, slight movements and signs of paranoia—side effects of what they've been through. She could only imagine what the campers might be like, considering the fact that they hadn't had the same number of years as these counselors to process everything.

Annie peeked at the little piece of paper as Jordan unfolded and read it aloud, "Max." Jordan looked up at him and smiled.

"All right, Max and Jordan, you two are a pair," Nick said, shaking the hat, shuffling the papers around inside.

Max nodded with a frown.

"Don't get too excited about it," Jordan said.

"No, it's not that I'm not willing to work with you. I just kind of pictured working with Casey this summer," Max said.

"God, get over it." Vera crashed her palm onto her forehead. Max looked at her like he thought of something mean to say but chose not to.

Jordan rose from her seat next to Annie and made her way over to Max. She managed to fit herself onto the log, with only half of a butt cheek resting on it. Eventually, George vacated the log, allowing Max to scoot over and create more space for her.

"Well Casey may not be here this summer, but I'm the next best thing, so don't be so gloomy."

Annie thought it sounded funny coming from her, as Jordan seemed like the personification of gloom, but it was good to see that she was turning out to be a nice girl. Much nicer than Vera, at least.

Max looked down at his hip that was now rubbing against Jordan's, and he seemed to be embarrassed, nervous, and excited all at once. "It'll be fun," he muttered and swallowed.

"Next," Nick said, holding the hat beside Annie's cheek. She could see how it might've made Jordan uncomfortable. It felt invasive.

She turned the same way Jordan did and reached her hand inside, shuffling the two pieces of papers left inside between her fingers, feeling for which one might call her name more. She thought of the two remaining candidates, and while she didn't know either of them particularly well, she thought of which one she was more interested in spending the rest of the summer getting to know.

George was a looker. With his sun-kissed flesh tone, his sharp jawline, his deep blue eyes, the way his clothes appeared tailored to be just tight enough to show off his sculpted form, and the way he somehow smelled great even though he always appeared to have sweat in the right spots to give him a bit of a shine—like he'd just oiled himself up. Not to mention his big, toned forearms. Annie had a thing for guys with big forearms.

Neil was the opposite of George. Not that he was ugly or anything. That wouldn't matter to Annie since she wasn't here looking for a boyfriend, but he wasn't an eye magnet in the same way George was. And from the little bit she'd seen of him, he was clearly lazy and she didn't want to be stuck doing all the work while he just sat around. And she was worried about his potential hygiene issue. There is nothing worse than a guy who smells when they have done nothing all day. It's a big red flag.

Although she knew she wasn't here to find a boyfriend and wasn't even contemplating it at the moment, she couldn't help but be drawn to the guy who resembled someone right out of her wildest dreams. However, this didn't mean she wouldn't be open to the possibility if his personality were to match his appearance.

George, George, George, she thought as she grabbed that last piece of paper. She felt all eyes on her while she held it in her hand and brought it down to her knees, waiting to open it. "So as cabin leaders, are we required to sleep in the same cabin as our campers?" she asked, because the sudden thought of sharing a cabin with Neil for the whole simmer made her queasy.

"No. We leave the cabins to the campers—give them a sense of freedom, you know?" Mitch said.

"The counselors have their own cabin," Nick added.

Great, she thought. She would still have to sleep near Neil, but at least she would have girls her age nearby; their perfume should be enough to mask the man stench. Hopefully, anyway.

After she stopped procrastinating, she unfolded the sheet of paper. "George," she read out loud with a sigh of relief.

He smiled at her and took a seat beside her. "This should be fun," he said.

She wasn't sure what he meant by it, as in whether he actually meant it or if it was just sarcasm, but she didn't think too deep about it.

"So that leaves Neil and Jenna," Nick stated, dumping the last sheet of paper still in the hat, presumably with Neil's name written on it, into the fire.

Jenna waved to Neil, and he waved back. He seemed happy.

"Remember, there is no swapping once the campers get here, so if you have a problem with this, speak up now," Nick said, waiting for an answer. But everyone seemed fine with their selections.

Thank God, Annie thought, worried that Jenna might complain about working with Neil and she'd get stuck with him.

"Then that's it for official counselor business," Nick declared, taking his seat at the fire once more.

"Wait, that's it?" Max asked.

"Well we still need to show Annie where the counselors' cabin is and get fully prepared for tomorrow, but we've covered all the basic job instructions. Plus, I'm afraid I've got an early morning tomorrow. I need to go with Betty on the bus to collect some campers." Mitch wheeled himself away from the fire. "But you guys hang out as long as you want. Just remember, you have an early day tomorrow too.

Try to get some sleep." The counselors watched him wheel his chair to the cafeteria.

Nick yawned. "I'm gonna get some sleep. You guys should know where the counselors' cabin is. Make sure you get your bags from the cafeteria and show Annie where it is. The beds aren't assigned, so you can all pick where you want to sleep. Just don't be loud when you come in."

Chapter 4

They didn't stay at the fire for too much longer, as they were all tired from the day's work. Jenna helped Annie carry her bags to the counselors' cabin, which was on the opposite side of the cafeteria building from the firepit.

Annie observed that this cabin was approximately half the size of the others, which Jenna mentioned would be used as the campers' sleeping quarters. However, upon entering, Annie realized that the interior was more than spacious enough to accommodate the eight counselors. The cabin welcomed Annie with one large room adorned with quaint knit rugs, two slightly worn-out couches, and a deer head mounted above a brick fireplace on the right wall near the entrance. Annie couldn't determine if the trophy was real or not.

In the room's corner, just behind the fireplace, was a small kitchen counter with a sink, a stack of clean ceramic plates, a dish drying rack, and a small microwave. Sitting below the counter was a mini refrigerator and a metal bucket lined with a grocery bag—a makeshift garbage bin.

Arranged along the left wall, opposite the fireplace, were five sets of bunk beds. The idea of the lifeless deer observing Annie as she slept sent a chill down her spine. Positioned between the beds and the kitchen counter on the back wall was a lengthy dresser, which she presumed they would all share during the summer. She felt relieved that she had packed minimally, as there was simply no room for all their clothes otherwise.

The dim glow in the room came from a single light hanging from the center of the ceiling that shook as the fan connected to it spun in vicious circles.

Though it hadn't taken long for them to reach the cabin, Nick was already in a deep sleep—accentuated by his loud, open-mouth snoring—on the top bunk in the back corner of the room. His belongings remained neatly in his open duffle bag between the bed and dresser.

The rest of the guys were quick to pick their beds. Neil took the bunk below Nick's, George took the top bunk of the bed closest to theirs, and Max took the bottom bunk of the bed next in line, leaving only the two closest beds to the door completely empty.

"Do you want the top or the bottom?" Jenna asked, her hand on one of the empty bedposts.

"Huh?" Annie looked at her until she realized it was an offer. She considered the other beds available but was happy to bunk with Jenna. She wasn't sure she was comfortable with any of the other counselors yet, but she got along with Jenna. "Oh, either is fine."

"Then you can have the bottom. If some stranger comes in here with a knife, they'll go after you first."

Annie found herself uncertain about how to react. It seemed like a joke, but given the collective experiences of everyone in the room, Annie couldn't find it in herself to laugh. She expected Jenna to acknowledge the impact of her words, feel remorseful, and apologize to each person individually. However, to Annie's surprise, no one seemed to react at all.

"She's right." Jordan nonchalantly entered the room and placed her bags on the top bunk of the second empty bed, stating, "Usually, the top bunk is reserved for concealing bodies." She climbed up the small ladder, leaving her shoes at the bottom, and crawled into bed.

Annie narrowed her eyebrows.

"She's just joking," Jenna said.

"Yeah, she spends too much time watching those slasher movies," Vera added, digging through her suitcase for clothes to sleep in.

"Besides, if someone came into this room with a knife, I'd handle them," George assured from his top bunk, legs dangling in front of Vera like a curtain. He flexed his right bicep and kissed it.

"You'd be the first to die. Haven't you seen a slasher movie?" Jordan asked.

"She's right," Jenna said.

Vera and Max nodded.

"Seen one? Shit, I survived one," George said.

"You were a background character, if anything." Vera laughed.

"As if. More like the hero."

"You didn't even know what was going on until it was over."

"So what?"

"I'm sorry, what happened?" Annie asked. "I don't mean to be intrusive, but you seem comfortable enough to be talking about it anyway."

"Don't be sorry. Mitch does great things at this camp. He taught us to get over our issues and not let them control us—even laugh about them when we can. And it just so happens that my story is the most laughable," George said.

"That's not true," Vera chimed in, her eyes pointing darts at Neil.

"I don't think any of the stories are funny. Not when you consider the people that died," Neil stated quietly from his bunk. Annie felt a shift in the air, as if all the happiness of the night was sucked out of the room.

George ran his tongue over his top row of teeth and brought his eyes back to Annie. He cleared his throat and said, "During my sophomore year of high school, a former student showed up at the homecoming dance with a ski mask and a knife. He went on a stabbing spree, injuring twelve and . . . murdering eight others."

"But George here stopped him," Vera interjected, slapping his calf. Annie knew she was trying to make him feel better. The joking was over. Neil took the enjoyment from them.

"How'd you stop him?" Annie asked, thinking it would cheer him up.

"Like Vera said, I was basically a background character. He had already finished his spree and was preparing to escape. He dumped the knife and mask in the boys' bathroom garbage can and tried to hustle out of the school. On his way across the dance floor, he bumped into me and scuffed my shoe. I was wearing a brand new pair of Jordans I'd bought specifically for that dance." George brought his legs up onto the bunk and lay down. "It pissed me off. Probably more than it should have. I yelled at him. He told me to fuck off. That just made me madder, so I hit him. One punch was all it took. He was a small guy, so he fell to the floor and hit his head—knocked him unconscious. When the cops arrived, I was sure they were gonna peg me for assault, but a witness who saw him dumping the knife in the bathroom told the cops what happened. The guy still had blood on his hands, and he eventually admitted to those murders." George started shaking just thinking about it.

"It sounds to me like you're a hero," Annie said.

"And a lucky one at that. You didn't have to go through the terrible nights, being chased all the while feeling so helpless. As far as you were aware, the worst night of your life was over as soon as it started," Vera said. Annie knew she was still trying to comfort George by the change in her tone from when they were teasing each other earlier.

Annie was intrigued by the fact that even though Vera couldn't see him in the bunk above hers, she could sense that he wasn't in a good state of mind. While Annie was glad to listen to the survivors' stories, she couldn't help but feel a sense of displacement. It was as if she didn't belong there, working alongside these individuals who had experienced so much while she had led a safe and content life in comparison. At the very least, she shared this feeling with Nick.

"So—and please forgive me if I'm overstepping here—if you weren't aware of what was going on until it was over, why did you come to this camp? It's not like you witnessed any of the murders." George sat up from the mattress, and Annie felt the need to rephrase, to not sound so completely ignorant. "I only ask so I can get an idea of what I might work with when it comes to the campers. I just want a better understanding of the trauma you've experienced."

"Survivor's guilt." George lay back down, his hands clasped under his head. "I know now that there was nothing more I could do, but convincing my subconscious to believe that is beyond difficult. I was at that dance, same as everyone. And clearly, I was strong enough to stop the asshole. If I had just gotten to him sooner, people would still be alive. Good people. Holding that feeling with me through high school was rough. I became depressed and felt like I didn't deserve to live a happy or successful life since those seven kids and one teacher who died couldn't. I saw all of their faces from their memorial pictures in my mind every night for a whole year following the event. It wasn't until I came here that I was able to tell myself that I did all I could and that some people were just awful. That man brought a knife to a social event and took innocent lives. I constantly tell myself that he took enough from this earth that day, and he doesn't deserve to take any more energy from my life."

"Wow," Annie said, because there wasn't much more she could say.

"Tough stuff, huh?" "Get used to it. You're gonna hear a lot of shit from these campers. You'll realize very quickly how dark this world can be." Jordan pulled out a journal and a pen from her bag.

"I think that's enough darkness for one night," Jenna said. "How about you grab your PJs and I'll show you where the showers are?"

"I was planning on showering in the morning," Annie said.

"That would be the smart thing to do. Everyone knows nighttime showers are ground zero for slasher victims," Jordan declared.

"Oh hush," Vera chided, getting out of her bed, pajamas in hand. "No more movies for you."

"Don't say I didn't warn you."

"I'm with Jordan," Annie said. If showering didn't already make her vulnerable enough, doing it at night in the middle of the woods sounded even less inviting.

"Nonsense, you'll be fine. Trust me. Besides, you'll be wanting to take your showers at night once the campers are here. Us girls have to wait for the teenage boys raging with hormones to go to sleep, otherwise, they'll try to sneak a peek. I have experienced that firsthand," Jenna said, looking at George.

"I told you already: I tossed my Frisbee too hard. I wasn't over there on purpose!" George said, yawning.

"You didn't even have a Frisbee!"

"I couldn't see where it went!"

"No, but you saw something much better."

"I sure as hell didn't want to play with Frisbees anymore." He smirked.

"Gross!" Vera yelled, grabbed her pillow, and hit him with it, bringing a laugh.

Jordan rolled her eyes. "I don't know about you, but I've suffered enough trauma in my life. I don't need kids spying on me too. I'll take a dimly lit night shower any day."

"You know, I think you've convinced me." Annie laughed and grabbed her pajamas and toiletry bag, which contained her body wash, hair products, mouthwash, toothbrush, and toothpaste, among other things.

"Ready to go?" Vera asked.

"Yep," Jenna said.

"Lead the way." Annie followed.

Chapter 5

Vera and Jordan guided Annie farther into the dense woods, venturing beyond the counselors' cabin and far from the campsite. Their path led them to a weathered, wooden structure stretching out before them. Inside, a solitary white light that flickered intermittently hung above the entrance, casting a dim glow. The buzzing of mosquitoes and the fluttering of moths filled the air, drawn to the erratic light.

"Does it always do that?" Annie asked.

"Only when you're most scared," Jenna joked. "Come on inside." She held the door open for them while Vera entered first and turned on the interior light with the timed dial beside the entrance. Annie set the dial for the maximum sixty minutes allowed, as she didn't want the light to go off while she was showering.

The bathroom had a dull and unsettling atmosphere, illuminated by bright blue tinted lighting. Along the left wall, there were six standing sinks emerging from the stone flooring. Each sink had a mirror behind it, with varying degrees of reflectiveness due to the unique patterns of cloudy fog that had accumulated over the years. These mirrors were attached to a wall made of tan wooden slats. Between the third and fourth sinks, there was a long counter that lacked a mirror, which struck Annie as rather odd. It also appeared to be about a foot shorter than the usual size, which mildly annoyed her. Across from the row of sinks, there were eight stalls, each enclosed by a flimsy, slightly opaque shower curtain. Suspended from the ceiling above each stall were rusty square shower heads, accompanied by a long chain hanging beside them.

"This is the 'counselors only' bathroom," Jenna said, leading the way to the counter where she placed her pajama set down. "So if you see any kids around here, they are either very lost or they are trying to invade our privacy."

"Okay. I noticed there wasn't a gender sign on the door, and this building didn't look big enough for another set of showers. Does that mean—"

Jenna cut off Annie's question before she could finish it. "Yep, we have to share with the boys. But they know good and well not to come in when we are here, especially if we claim it at night. If they do, just report it to . . . well, your granddad."

"The only one you have to worry about is George. Neil doesn't smell like he showers very often anyway. And Max and Nick are such virgins that I'm not convinced they really even like women," Vera said, placing her pajamas on the counter beside Jenna's and pulling her hair out of its messy bun.

"Geez, Vera."

"You really think so? Max seemed really upset about that Casey girl," Annie said.

"They had a fake relationship for a few years. As far as we know, she was just his beard, but who am I to judge?"

"Hey, didn't Nick ask you out before?" Jenna asked.

"Oh yeah. Huh," Vera said.

"Did that not convince you he liked women?"

"That doesn't mean anything. Have you seen me? It doesn't matter what or who you're into. I'm hot."

"All the more reason for people to want to spy on you, right?" Annie asked.

"Oh no," Jenna said. "I didn't grab a pair of panties."

Vera stopped as she was just about to pull her shirt off over her head. "Seriously?"

"Yeah, can you just walk back with me?"

Vera sighed. "Yeah, but let's hurry. I don't want to stay up too late."

"I'll go with you guys!" Annie said. She was offering more because she didn't want to be left alone, than to be actually helpful.

"That's okay. We'll be real quick." Jenna squatted and pointed below the counter. "The towels are all right here and there's a bin over there." She pointed to the corner of the room, between the shower stalls and the door. "Put your dirty towels in it and we will wash them every week."

"You're seriously gonna leave me here?"

"What, are you scared?" Vera laughed.

"Don't worry! I promise we'll be fast." Jenna grabbed Vera's hand and pulled her out of the bathroom.

Annie found herself all alone, with only the sound of the ticking, timed light switch. She placed her clothes on the counter next to Vera's and cautiously approached it, turning the dial to the maximum once again, just to be safe. She peered out of the bathroom door, hoping to glimpse the girls approaching the cabin. But the woods appeared as dark as an endless void since the outside light had burnt out while she was inside. A wave of unease washed over her, causing her to retreat into the bathroom. Returning to the counter, she kicked off her shoes, removed her socks, and tucked them inside her shoes before placing them on the counter. She then undressed, pausing momentarily before unhooking her bra to scan her surroundings and ensure no one was watching. Even though she knew she was alone and no campers had arrived yet, the multiple mentions of Peeping Toms had made her extra vigilant.

Once she felt secure enough, she dropped her bra and her panties followed. She reached for a towel beneath the counter, but it felt flimsy and inadequate as she loosely wrapped it around her body, barely covering her most private areas. She then rummaged through her toiletry bag and retrieved her body wash, shampoo, and conditioner. In a hurry, she entered the third shower stall closest to the door. As she stepped over the small lip meant to keep the water inside, she saw that the floor was already wet, suggesting someone had recently used it. She didn't dwell on it since any of the other counselors, Betty, or the camp nurse could have used it before her. The only discomfort she felt stemmed from the gross sensation of the old, freezing water against her toes as she put her feet down.

Reluctantly, she finished stepping into the stall, hung her towel over the curtain rod, and placed her shower products in the corner on the floor. Then she pulled the curtain back to look out once again, half-checking for the other girls and half-checking for perverts. After confirming she was still alone, she turned and examined the pull chain for the showerhead hanging at shoulder height. It was a rusty silver, matching the showerhead, and had a black handle on its end. She grasped the handle and tugged, releasing a torrent of freezing water that splashed over her, sending shivers down her spine and forcing her to scurry to the corner of the stall.

I guess I'll have to wait until it warms up, she thought, rubbing her arms, jumping at every drop of water that splashed onto her naked body. After about twenty seconds went by, she reached into the water, and it was still just as cold. Then, the water stopped pouring.

"What the fuck?" her voice echoed within the stall. She looked through the curtain to see if the girls came back to pull a prank on her, but she was still alone. When she pulled the handle again, she stood outside of the water's path to watch it pour down. She didn't need to touch the water; she could feel from the humidity in the air that it wasn't getting any warmer. And after another thirty seconds, the water turned off again.

Great, she thought, and reached for the handle again, but before she could pull it, she heard a noise. It wasn't anything loud or particularly alarming, just a crack or a pop from the other side of the wall, just outside the building.

It could have been anything, really, but Annie struggled to convince herself of that. She was in the woods, fully aware that any animal could be lurking outside or a branch might have fallen from a tree. Even the rustling of the wind in the bushes played in her mind. However, what intensified her fear was the unsettling thought of someone spying on her. Sure, it would be repulsive if it were George, Neil, Max, or Nick, but at least she knew them. But what if it was an unfamiliar face peering in from the darkness?

Perversion is one thing, but why would somebody else be here at this time? It's not like this person would've known that she would take a shower here this late, or that they would've even known it was a bathroom to begin with. Unless, an even scarier thought, this person was waiting in the woods for a moment like this. They could've been hiking, stumbled upon the camp, seen the pretty girl counselors who work here, found the bathroom, and waited in the forest, watching for when they would come and disrobe. And what if they saw the three of them enter the bathroom, but only two of them leave? This man, whoever it could be, would know that she was alone.

Just at the peak of Annie's mental spiraling, right when she felt the most vulnerable, she heard the bathroom door creak open in a way it only would if the person opening it didn't want the person inside to know they were coming in. Annie first just listened, hoping to hear Vera or Jenna say something—anything—but they didn't. Her shower water was still off, so she didn't want to make a noise and let the intruder know she was in there. But the memory of putting her clothes on the counter replayed in her mind, and she realized it would be obvious to this person that not only was somebody else in the bathroom, they were nude.

"Hello?" Annie called out, deciding that there was nothing more she could do. If it was one of the girls, they would announce themselves, and if not, hopefully, one of the boys would leave. Instead of a vocal response, all she heard was light footsteps beneath the ticking of the light switch timer. Annie balled her fists and mouthed the word, "Fuck."

She peeled back the curtain to peek into the bathroom, making sure she was still covering herself. *Partially useless,* she thought, as the curtain was semi-transparent anyway. When she couldn't see anybody, she took a deep breath and forced her entire head out of the shower to look both ways and saw that she was still alone.

Either they left, or I'm going crazy— Her own screaming interrupted her thoughts as she heard a noise from inside her shower stall this time—a clap on the stone floor. She dropped to her knees, helpless as ever, crawled into the corner and cowered in the fetal position, continuing to scream as if someone had hacked their way through the wall with an axe and she was a targeted victim. Once she got over the initial shock, she saw that all the walls were still intact, as was her flesh, and that she was still alone in the stall. This was when she stopped screaming, heard the laughter, and looked up.

Jenna was peeking over the stall wall from the next shower over, laughing hysterically. Vera must've been in the same stall with her, as she was also laughing but out of sight. "I'm so sorry!" Jenna said, though her laughing didn't feel very apologetic to Annie. "I didn't think you'd get so scared!"

"What the fuck, guys?" Annie stood up, covering her chest with her right arm and pushing off the ground with her left.

"Vera thought it would be funny to scare you."

"And I was right!" Vera appeared, pulling aside Annie's curtain.

"Hey, I'm naked in here," Annie said, turning around to hide herself.

"Right, sorry," Jenna apologized, hopping down from whatever she stood on to peek over the wall.

"Oh my God, look at your face!" Vera pointed at Annie, who was turning her head back to look at her.

"Are you sure that's what you're looking—"

"You look like you've seen a ghost!" Vera interrupted.

"Yeah, you guys scared the shit out of me!"

"Can you give me my shoe back?" Vera held her hand out, as if saying, "Hand it here."

Annie looked down at her feet and saw the flip-flop between them. This was what they used to make the clapping sound. Jenna must have dropped it over the wall. Annie squatted to pick it up and passive-aggressively smacked it into Vera's hand.

"Thanks, babe," Vera said before disappearing behind the curtain. Annie saw her silhouette on the other side throw the sandal toward the counter before pulling her shirt off and unhooking her bra.

"Seriously, we're sorry," Jenna repeated.

"She is, at least," Vera said. "I have no regrets."

"How about you make it up to me and tell me how to get this shower to work?" Annie pulled the chain, stepping out of the water's path again.

"Oh right. I don't miss these things," Jenna said. Annie heard her stepping into the shower stall beside hers, the same one she used to scare her. "When you pull the chain, the water runs for a short time, but I'm sure you figured that out by now. Just pull it when you need water. Rinse, lather, rinse, and done. Not much more to it than that."

"Okay, but how do you get the water to warm up?"

Vera giggled as she entered the stall on the other side of Annie's. "You don't."

Annie watches the chain in Jenna's stall as she pulls it, releasing the water. "Seriously?"

"Seriously." Vera pulls her chain and the water stream follows.

"They seriously expect us to take cold showers all summer?" Annie asks.

"Ask your grandpa," Vera said.

"Sometimes the water warms up on a hot day, but we are usually working during those hours. And like we said before, you don't really want to take daytime showers unless you're willing to risk some little perverts peeping on you," Jenna said.

Annie considered this, then thought of how terrified the idea of someone spying on her made her feel tonight, then sighed before stepping underneath the cold water, accepting her fate. "I'll talk to Mitch."

"Hopefully you can talk some sense into him," Vera said, the water splashing about her as Annie imagined it running through her hair. "We've been complaining about it for years."

Annie's water stopped, leaving her even colder as the air touched her wet skin. She hurried to squirt body wash into her hands and lather up her body. Then she pulled the string as Jenna's water stopped and rinsed herself off.

Their showers only lasted a couple more minutes—the exact opposite of Annie's usual overly long shower habits—as none of them had any need or want to stay under that freezing water longer than necessary. Annie pulled her towel down, furiously rubbed it against her body, and tied it around herself before stepping out.

She looked to her side and noticed a shower chair outside of Jenna's stall. Had to be what she stood on to peek over the wall. She walked to the counter as the other girls stepped out of their showers one at a time and joined her at the counter where they all put their pajamas on.

Annie's were a matching set—green satin shorts and a button-up top. Vera wore red flannel pajama bottoms with a maroon tank top, and Jenna wore a gray onesie.

"Wait, you guys didn't have those when we first came here!" Annie said, pointing at the slippers Jenna was putting on and Vera's flip-flops.

"Oh yeah, we grabbed them when we went back to the cabin," Jenna said. "We didn't want to walk through the woods barefoot on the way back."

"I didn't even think about it," Annie said. She hadn't brought a clean pair of socks to put on after the shower, and she would not put on the old pair. Having to choose between which was more gross, she waited for the girls to be ready to leave before slipping her bare feet into her sneakers and following them back into the darkness of the woods.

"At least it's not a long walk," Jenna said. Annie appreciated the optimism, but she was still uncomfortable.

"Yeah, that's true, I guess."

"Wait, who's that?" Vera asked. Annie looked up from her shoes in the direction Vera was now pointing and saw a silhouette approaching them, becoming clearer as Annie's eyes focused on the shadow.

"Jordan?" Jenna guessed, recognizing her much faster than Annie could.

"What are you doing out here?" Vera asked.

"George's snoring was keeping me awake, so I thought a shower didn't sound so bad." Jordan had already put on her sleep clothes—an oversized Metallica T-shirt and no pants. She looked just as tough as usual, even with her dark eye makeup and lipstick removed, thanks to her messy hairdo. In contrast, she wore pink bunny slippers that gave her a cute, innocent side in Annie's eyes.

"Ew, he's a snorer?" Vera asked, and Jordan nodded.

"But what about the slasher rules? You're gonna be all alone in there!" Jenna crept slowly to Jordan, wiggling her fingers for dramatic, scary effect.

"Oh please, I'll take my chances with a perverted serial killer any day over the snoring monster in that cabin," Jordan said, and all the girls laughed.

"Well, good luck in there! Scream as loud as you can to excite the killer while he's slashing you up!" Vera said.

"Yeah, I'll make sure to spend some extra time soaping up my breasts to get him excited beforehand." Jordan gave them a thumbs-up, then continued on her way.

"She's funny," Annie said, bringing her eyes back down to her shoes as they walked.

"It comes and goes. She can be a real bitch, trust me," Vera said.

"So can you!" Jenna yelled.

"Can be? I'm always a bitch."

"At least you're aware of it."

"Exactly."

They got back to the counselors' cabin shortly after. It was much darker than when they left without the interior lights pouring out of the windows. Vera shushed Jenna as she pulled the door open and it let out a loud creak. George's snoring welcomed them as soon as they stepped inside.

"She wasn't joking," Annie whispered.

"We're gonna have to cover our ears with our pillows," Jenna said.

"Or I'll just cover his face with one," Vera joked, warranting a laugh from the other girls, who quickly hushed when they heard Nick roll over in his bed.

Annie followed Jenna to their bunk bed in the corner and waited for her to climb up the ladder before squeezing between it and the wall to crawl under her blankets. The bed wasn't the most comfortable she had ever slept in, but the warm scent of woodsmoke lingering in the air gave her a sense of coziness that reminded her of cold winter nights by the fireplace—nights she would dream of once she drifted off to sleep.

Chapter 6

Annie found herself abruptly awakened by the distant, frantic ringing of bells. The counselors she bunked with reacted with gasps, groans, and yawns. She lay in bed, pretending she had heard nothing.

"So soon?" Jenna asked from above her.

"There's no way," George said.

"Ugh!" Vera yelled into her pillow.

Jenna rustled about in her bunk while Annie struggled to open her eyes. The sun hadn't risen enough to let any significant light into their cabin through the window. Annie's view was limited to Jenna's dangling feet as she sat on the edge of her bed, let out a small squeak as she finished yawning, then descended the wooden ladder to the floor. Rubbing her eyes, she made her way to the door and flicked on the light switch, which caused more groans from Jordan and Max.

"Fine, I'll get up," Max grumbled.

"At least warn me before you turn on the light," Jordan whined, pulling her blanket over her head.

"Whoa, Jordan made it through the night alive, you guys," Vera said.

"Waking up this early, I wish I didn't." She threw her blanket off and sat up straight, looking around the room. "Where's Nick?"

"He's not in his bed?" Annie asked, getting out of bed and peeking over.

"I'll bet he's the one ringing that bell out there," George said.

"Doesn't Mitch usually do that?" Max asked.

"Yeah, but Nick is being such a teacher's pet . . . it wouldn't surprise me," Vera said.

"So wh—" Max stopped mid-sentence at the sound of a light snore in the room's corner. "Is Neil still sleeping?"

Everyone looked over at him, and he was dead asleep. Annie giggled, but everyone else either rolled their eyes or sighed. They were all fed up with his laziness.

"Time to wake up, buddy," George said as he sat shirtless on his bed, tossing his pillow down onto Neil's face, who jumped up like he was having a nightmare.

"Whoa, wait, wha—" Neil muttered frantically, looking around the room until he remembered where he was. "What's going on?"

"Time to wake up," Vera said.

"What time is it?"

"Who knows? We don't have our phones." Vera got out of bed and walked to the kitchen sink. Everyone just watched—they were too tired to do anything else—as she turned it on and started splashing her face.

"Oh, that reminds me," Max said. "Do you think we have time to take a shower before they put us to work?"

Vera turned to him from the sink. "Time or not, you're showering. I don't want to smell you." She turned and pointed at the other guys in the room and said, "And that goes for all of you." Annie saw a tad more emphasis when she pointed in Neil's direction. She felt bad, but maybe it was for the best. "Nick, too, if he didn't shower already." Vera turned back to the sink slowly, as if disgusted with the boys, then jumped back, yelping, "OH MY GOD!" She covered her mouth and pointed toward the sink.

George leapt down from his bed and put his arms around her, looking toward the sink. "What, what is it?"

The rest of the counselors watched, interested and slightly concerned about what would frighten her so much.

"There, under the sink," she said, her arm shaking. She dropped to the floor as soon as George let her go to inspect.

He bent over, keeping his distance at first, then got real close and crouched to get a better view. "I don't see any—Shit!" He fell on his ass and crawled backward faster than Annie had seen anybody do before, as a large wolf spider scurried across the floor toward him. He leaned forward, balled his fist, and slammed it onto the floor repeatedly, all while sharing screams with Vera until they were sure there was no more movement from it.

"Did you get it?" Vera asked.

"I think so." George lifted his hand, revealing a big, circular dark spot on the floor with the spider's legs sticking straight up, twitching as they shrunk to the floor. George looked at his hand and gagged at the spider's remains stuck to it.

"Ew!" Vera yelled when she saw it. "Go wash your hands."

George stood and walked to the sink, avoiding stepping on the spot he left on the floor, turned it on and rinsed off his hand.

"If that's how you react to a poor little spider, I can't wait until a killer walks through our door," Jordan joked.

"Hey, I still killed it, didn't I? I didn't see any of you jumping to Vera's rescue." George finished washing his hands, shut the sink off, then dried his hands with a paper towel from the roll hanging on the wall behind the sink.

"Maybe we just didn't think a teensy spider was so urgent." Jordan descended the bunk ladder and walked to her bag on the dresser. "Either way, us girls need to get dressed, so you boys can go take your showers now. Nick's probably gonna freak out if we take any longer to get to work."

"Oh, and don't forget," Jenna chimed in, "we are meeting the campers for the first time today! Make sure you all put on your uniforms."

Annie followed the other girls to the campfire where Nick stood impatiently, arms crossed, beside the flagpole with the bell he had been ringing all morning connected to it.

"Finally!" he yelled, throwing his hands up when he saw them. "What took you guys so long?"

"Calm down," Jordan said, "we had to put our clothes on and brush our teeth. You know, hygiene stuff."

"And there was a spider," Vera said.

"A spider?"

"Yeah, a really big one."

"It just about scared Vera out of her skin," Jenna said.

"Until George came to the rescue," Jordan teased.

"You guys were late over a spider?" Nick asked. "Where are the guys?"

"In the shower," Jenna said.

"You should join them," Vera stated.

He glared at her, annoyed at them being late, rather than at the suggestion. "I showered about an hour ago. Come on, we'd better get started before the kids get here."

They followed him into the large building that Annie knew was the cafeteria, past the rows of tables, past the entrance into the kitchen, and stopped at a door in the back right corner of the building. Nailed onto the wall above it was a rectangular piece of wood that read *NURSE'S OFFICE.*

Nick politely knocked on the door before opening it, allowing them to enter the small, square-shaped office. Inside, a bookshelf occupied one wall, displaying several medical guides alongside a solitary rose delicately placed in a mason jar filled with water. Two picture frames caught Annie's eye, one featuring a man and the other showcasing a beloved dog. Familiar romance and dark fantasy novels instantly recognizable to Annie also lined the shelves. Adjacent to the wall, an office desk stood with a lonely laptop perched on it. In the far corner of the room on the right-hand side, a five-drawer vertical filing cabinet stood, topped by a lavender-colored suitcase and duffle bag. On the wall to the right, an open medicine cabinet hung, containing only a few essential first aid items.

Seated at the desk was a woman in her late twenties with loose, wavy brunette hair pulled back. She was dressed in yoga pants and a V-neck T-shirt. Her eyes appeared exhausted, mirroring the fatigue felt by everyone that morning. On the floor, completely unaware of their presence, lay the dog in the picture frame. Annie knew it was a mixed breed, resembling a corgi in the face and sharing the same coat color and pattern. However, it stood twice as tall and weighed significantly more, indicating that it was well-fed.

The woman sat up in her chair, adjusted her shirt, wiped her eyes, and worked up a smile for them. "Hey, everyone," she said, trying her best to sound enthusiastic. Her head tilted when she saw Annie. "I don't think I recognize you."

"I'm Annie, Mitch's granddaughter," she said, extending her hand.

The woman shook her hand. "Oh, that's right! He mentioned you. I'm Cherie, the camp nurse."

"Woodsby!" Jenna yelled, waking the dog that she approached and started petting.

"And this is Park Ranger Woodsby," Cherie said, smiling at the corgi.

"He's an emotional support dog. All the campers that come through here get to spend time with him, and they all love it. Especially Woodsby," Nick said.

"He's so cute," Annie said.

"Do you wanna meet him?" Jenna asked.

"Can I?"

Cherie nodded and moved her chair aside while Jenna stood up to make space for Annie to squat beside him. When Jenna stopped petting him, he looked up at her as if he wanted more, but instead, he just smiled and playfully rolled around on the wooden floor when Annie began rubbing his head.

"Who's a good boy?" Annie asked with her high-pitched, talking to a dog voice.

"He's the best," Jenna said, kneeling back down to pet him some more.

"What's your story, little guy?" Annie asked, playfully scratching under his chin.

"Believe it or not, it's a similar one to the campers here," Cherie said.

"How do you mean?"

"Have you heard of Victoria Vance?" she asked.

Annie glanced at Jenna, her expression one of confusion. Jenna lowered her gaze and shook her head, as though the mere thought of the story was dreadful. She then shifted her attention to Nick, who wore a furious expression and clicked his teeth in annoyance.

"I'm sorry, I don't think I ever have," Annie said.

"She's just another name you can add to your shit list as you hear more and more stories this summer. But she's a real nasty one. Apparently, she came home one night with the intention of murdering her family. What she didn't know was that her little brother was sleeping at a friend's house down the street. She tortured her parents, trying to get them to tell her where he was, but they wouldn't budge, so she just killed them. Then she found her mom's planner at her bedside and saw *OLIVER'S SLEEPOVER* written on that very date. She knew he had a lot of friends who lived on their street but didn't know which house he was at, so she worked her way through the neighborhood, going house to house and leaving a blood trail in her wake until she found her brother and killed him too," Cherie explained.

Annie gasped. "Oh my God. "But what about Woodsby?"

"He was the pet of that last family, the one whose house Victoria's little brother was sleeping at. Woodsby was just a puppy back then, but it was his barking that woke the folks in the last house on that street, and they called the police. When the first responders arrived, Oliver's friend was the only one still alive—having not yet succumbed to his throat being slit. Woodsby followed the boy as they put him on the stretcher and into the ambulance. They were in such a rush to get him to the hospital that they didn't bother trying to get Woodsby out of the vehicle. He waited patiently in the corner of the ambulance until they arrived and he followed them into the trauma unit where I was working. They wouldn't let him much farther inside, obviously, but my boss let me stay with him."

"Oh my God," Annie said, looking down at Woodsby. "I can't believe he went through all of that."

"I know. And unfortunately, they couldn't save that little boy. I couldn't let Woodsby go to the pound, hearing what happened to that poor family, so I took him in. When I was told I could come work at this summer camp, I asked if I could bring my dog. Mitch asked if I could train him to be an emotional support dog, and here we are."

"Wow. I'm really speechless," Annie said.

"It's okay, he speaks for himself. After everything, he's still so happy and full of life. And he gets to spend his time spreading that joy to other kids that went through terrible things, just like his original owner," Cherie said.

"Well now that you guys have met, we have some work we have to take care of before the campers get here," Nick said.

"Oh right," Annie said. She and Jenna gave Woodsby some final pets and stood up.

"It was nice to meet you. I'll be here all summer, so if you need anything, please feel free to ask. And never be afraid to send a kid my way if you're unsure of how to deal with them," Cherie said.

"Thank you."

Chapter 7

When Hailey saw the bus, it wasn't what she expected, but she wasn't sure what she was expecting. Someone had painted a forestry camouflage pattern on a regular school bus. She was hoping it wasn't her bus because she felt embarrassed even walking near it, but there was no mistaking it; it was hers because it had the words *CAMP SAFE WOODS* painted in bright red on both long sides of it, beneath the windows.

It was the last place she wanted to spend her summer vacation before her senior year, but her adoptive parents thought it was for the best after she got into a fight near the end of the school year. She thought she had good enough reason to fight this girl—she had made fun of her for being an orphan—but it just clicked in her parents' minds that she wasn't coping well with the things she'd seen, and the brochure for this camp must've looked like a winning lottery ticket to them.

As Hailey observed the other campers receiving warm embraces from their families, she couldn't help but notice how fortunate they were to have their loved ones personally drop them off at the station instead of relying on a taxi for the entire journey. Before boarding the bus, Hailey shared a heartfelt hug with Lana, her cherished stuffed Loch Ness Monster, a gift from her biological mother. Lana was her constant companion, providing comfort during times of loneliness. Over the years, Lana had become worn and damaged, a result of Hailey's restless nights filled with nightmares that left her with multiple stitches and a missing eye. Despite her appearance resembling something a creepy child from a horror movie would carry, Hailey didn't mind. In fact, she strongly identified with those children, feeling a deep connection to them.

There were campers of all ages, from grade school to borderline adulthood, like Hailey. Given the purpose of this camp, it hurt her heart to think that these elementary school-aged children would have to be sent to a place like this, but she understood childhood trauma all too well. She couldn't help but wonder if coming to a place like this earlier would have benefited her. At this stage of her life, she already felt as if she had moved on from it.

Placing Lana on top of her suitcase, she walked through the doors, up the steps, and turned past the bus driver, who was pleasantly plump. They shared a smile and a nod as their eyes met. The bus seemed much smaller inside compared to its appearance from the outside, likely due to the numerous campers occupying the space.

Walking down the narrow aisle, she accidentally bumped her suitcase against a seat in every other row. After making her way about three-quarters toward the back of the bus, she finally spotted an empty row. She pulled her luggage in behind her and sat down. Placing the suitcase between her legs, she settled in. But as she looked up, her heart skipped a beat—Lana was no longer resting on the luggage. Panic set in as she searched the seat beside her, the floor, the aisle, and then her eyes landed on the preppy blonde two rows ahead, across the center aisle. The girl held Lana in the air, laughing with those around her.

They must have grabbed her when I walked by, she thought. Stressing over what to say to them, she struggled to get her luggage out from in front of her so she could stand up. Before she could, she saw another girl, a brunette, come down the aisle and snatch Lana from the blonde's hands.

"Hey—" she yelled, but the brunette ignored her and looked straight at Hailey.

"This is yours, right?" she asked. The girl was pretty, with bronze skin and burnt orange eyes. Her hair curled in all the right places, leaving Hailey envious.

She swallowed the lump that developed in her throat and nodded. The girl looked back at the blonde—a dirty look, Hailey assumed—and proceeded to Hailey's row. She handed Lana to her.

"Thank you." Hailey put Lana back on her luggage and sat down.

"Don't mention it." The girl took the aisle seat next to Hailey, put her own backpack between her legs, and offered a handshake. "I'm Alejandra, but you can call me Ale."

"I'm Hailey." She took her hand and shook it.

Ale had a wide, contagious smile. "What's your story?"

Hailey pondered it, knowing that the inevitable moment would arrive when people would question her reasons for attending this camp. She spent hours contemplating what she would say to others, but she couldn't come up with an answer that they would find believable. She had shared her story with others in the past, only to be met with skeptical looks, unless they had heard her story through the news. In those cases, their expressions shifted from pity to excitement and curiosity, none of which she welcomed.

"You don't have to tell me if you don't want to. I get it," Ale said, cutting off the awkward silence Hailey gave her as a response. "This is my first time at a place like this, so I don't really know my boundaries just yet."

Hailey laughed. "It's my first year too. I didn't really wanna come to begin with, but my parents—"

"Oh, tell me about it," Ale interrupted. "I do not fit the description of the campers this place is meant to entertain. Traumatized, really?" She looked at Hailey and quickly erased the smile from her face. "Oh my gosh, I'm sorry. I'm not, like, making fun of people who are traumatized or anything."

"Don't worry about—"

"I was just saying that I'm not traumatized." She shifted in her seat. "Let me explain."

"It's fine, really—"

"I guess some lunatic went crazy at this county fair and attacked a bunch of people. One of my cousins died, the other remains missing. They caught the guy, and he tried saying that aliens did it. Can you believe that?"

Hailey puffed out her lower lip and shook her head.

"Anyway, I barely even knew my cousins. I mean, I would see them at the yearly family reunion, but we never spoke outside of that. My mom completely overreacted after the incident and decided we needed to move across the state to be closer to my aunt. And now she is projecting her own emotions onto me by sending me to this camp." She took a deep breath once she finished her story, as if she ran out of air telling it.

"Wow," Hailey said, afraid that Ale would interrupt again if she tried to get out another sentence.

They both turned their heads to face the back of the bus as electronic whirring lifted a wheelchair-bound man into the aisle from outside. He greeted the row of campers at the very back, wheeled himself to a comfortable position in the center of the bus, and cleared his throat.

When the bus didn't quiet down as he had planned, the driver yelled over the impressive intercom system, "Quiet down and listen up!"

"Thank you, Betty." The man began slowly wheeling himself down the aisle, nodding at each kid he locked eyes with as he spoke loud and clear, "My name is Mitch. Some of you know me already, and some of you" —he noticed and smiled at Hailey—"are new here. I am the founder and owner of Camp Safe Woods, and you are on my bus. If that doesn't sound correct to you, you are on the wrong bus and need to leave immediately." He waited a moment, looking around for anybody to take him up on that offer. "Nobody? Okay, then. Everybody is where they need to be. It is currently"—he pulled back his tattered denim jacket sleeve to look at his watch—"ten fifteen a.m., and I made it clear to your parents we would leave at ten ten. So, congratulations, you have all made it on time. Anyone who comes later . . . Well, they have a two-hour drive to the camp from here, and so do we! Now let's all please get along, introduce yourselves to each other, take a nap, and try not to be annoying. If any of you have to take a bathroom break, please let us know so we can pull over and find you a bush somewhere."

Eventually, he reached the front of the bus and then turned around to address the campers. "Any questions?" All the kids ignored him and went back to being loud and talking about random things as they were before Mitch boarded. "All right, off we go."

Betty started the bus and Mitch maneuvered himself from the wheelchair to the handicap seat just behind her.

"Do you think he meant that bush thing?" Ale asked. "I have a pretty small bladder."

"I hope not," Hailey said, adjusting Lana, who almost fell over once the bus's wheels started moving. "Thanks again. I don't remember if I said that before."

"Don't worry about it. Seriously, that girl was clearly being such a bitch and I am not excited to be spending the summer near her. We just have to make sure we don't let people like that walk all over us while we're here," Ale said.

"Yeah, seriously. I didn't even know she had grabbed her until I sat down."

Ale smiled. "Well us non-bitchy girls need to look out for each other while we're here."

"Definitely."

"So if you won't tell me *your* story, what about hers?" Ale pointed at Lana. "She's clearly been through a lot.

Hailey laughed. "She really has." She ran her finger across Lana's forehead as if petting it, while thinking back on things that she had gotten her through. "My mom gave her to me when I was a baby. She comes with me everywhere and reminds me of her."

"She passed away?"

Hailey nodded. "When I was a kid."

"Oh, I thought you said earlier your parents sent you—"

Hailey interrupted, saying, "I was adopted. My biological mom's best friend took me in after she died."

"So your dad . . .?"

"He's in prison. Has been since before I was born."

"That's fucked-up. What did he do?"

"Nothing. At least, that's what I think. He was wrongfully convicted."

"Oh my gosh."

"Well, I'm like seventy percent sure. Maybe sixty."

"That's not a high percentage."

"I know. I mean, I've looked into his case and I can see why they convicted him. The evidence all pointed to him, but when he told me his side of the story, I . . ."—Hailey looked to the ceiling as if she would find her next words up there—"I believe him."

"Oh, so you've met him?"

"Only through letters. We became pen pals last year."

Ale looked at her, skepticism written on her face. "Forgive me if I'm overstepping, but it would make sense for someone to at least try to convince their daughter that they didn't commit a crime."

"He doesn't know."

"What? What do you mean he doesn't know?"

"I never told him who I was. Hell, he doesn't even know he has a daughter. My mom never reached out to him when she found out she was pregnant. They were just a one-night fling, and they never saw each other again."

Ale's eyebrows raised.

"When I reached out to him, I wasn't sure if I wanted him to know about me or not. My mom didn't want him to for a reason, and I respected that, but I didn't like the idea that there weren't any other people on Earth who shared my blood that I could talk to, so I reached out. Just to see at first . . . find out who he was as a person. I wanted to give him a chance. But I remained anonymous," Hailey said.

"Okay, I guess I can understand that. What was he convicted of?"

"Murder."

Ale's jaw fell. "That's some dangerous stuff there, girl."

"I know, but like I said, he probably didn't do it."

Ale sat back in her seat and closed her eyes. "Your parents might've been on to something."

Hailey pulled her hair around her right shoulder and played with the ends. "What do you mean?"

"This place sounds perfect for someone who's been through as much as you have."

Hailey smiled. "You have no idea."

Chapter 8

Two hours and three bathroom breaks later—only one involving a bush—they arrived at camp. Hailey woke Ale from her nap to point out the big *CAMP SAFE WOODS* sign while all the other campers admired through the windows with audible oohs and ahhs.

The bus continued straight along the road for another quarter mile, passing a small parking lot. It then reached a fork, with one path leading left and the other right, both encircling a large open space ahead. In the middle of this space stood a big log building, a flagpole, another pole with a bell attached to a small rope, and an area designated for a campfire. Rather than choosing either direction at the fork, the bus drove straight ahead, traversing the dirt path until it came to a stop right in front of the campfire. Mitch, sitting in his wheelchair with a box on his lap, made his way to the back of the bus. He started descending down the wheelchair elevator while the campers hurriedly exited the bus. Just before leaving, Hailey noticed the blonde girl who had snatched Lana earlier giving both her and Ale disdainful glances.

"This summer's gonna be a lot of fun," Ale remarked, to which Hailey simply nodded and followed her off the bus.

At the campfire, the eight counselors stood proudly beneath a banner hanging between two distant ladders that read *WELCOME TO CAMP SAFE WOODS*. The campers wore silly uniforms: white T-shirts with the camp's logo across the chest and red accents around the sleeves, with booty shorts for the gals and Bermuda sorts for the guys. Hailey was quick to develop opinions on the female counselors based on how they wore those uniforms. Primarily the one girl who tied her shirt above her belly so it was more of a crop top and pulled her shorts up higher than they needed to be. Hailey shivered at the thought of the wedgie the girl must have had.

Mitch rolled his chair over to the counselors and began handing them name tags from the box in his lap. They took them and pinned them onto the left side of their shirts. Hailey, still fixating on the girl with the extra-skimpy outfit, squinted to read her name tag: *VERA*. The silhouette of an eagle decorated it, just above her name.

"I'm sure glad we don't have to wear outfits like those," Ale said, slightly startling Hailey, who had forgotten she was standing beside her.

"I wouldn't be so sure," said a voice from behind them. They turned around and saw a nerdy-looking boy who was about the same age as them. They both stared at him, waiting for him to elaborate. "It's kind of required here. I'm not sure if your parents told you, but they definitely bought a uniform for you."

"Ew," Ale said. "Well I guess they're not that bad. He looks pretty damn good in it." She nodded her head toward the fit male counselor, whose pectoral muscles were practically visible through his white shirt. Hailey focused on his name tag, which said *GEORGE* and had the silhouette of a squirrel above his name.

"I'm Billy, by the way."

"I'm Ale."

"And I'm Hailey."

"So you've been here before?" Ale asked.

"Yeah, this is my second year."

"And? How is it?"

"It's . . . an experience. That's for sure." He slung his drawstring bag over his shoulder.

"What do you mean?" Hailey asked.

"Well, it's helpful for those of us who need it. And it could be a lot of fun, but it's very hard to shake the overhanging cloud of gloom surrounding the place."

"I can see that. I've kind of felt that since I got on the bus," Hailey said.

"Cloud of gloom? What are you guys talking about?"

"Think about it," Billy said. "All of these campers here,"—he waved around at the dozens of kids surrounding them—"they've all been surrounded by death in some form or another."

Ale took quick glances at the campers. "Wow, that's . . . dark."

"Yeah." Billy laughed. "Don't get me wrong, we do some fun stuff at camp, but no matter how happy you are or how hard you're laughing, you'll eventually look over at another kid who isn't in the same mood. That kind of thing really bums you out. And that's not to mention how hard it is to sleep at night when someone in your cabin wakes up screaming from night terrors."

"Night terrors are real?" Ale asked, her eyes wide.

"Yeah, and they suck," Hailey said. "I've had them since I was ten."

"I used to have them, as well," Billy shared, "but I was lucky. They actually stopped after my first year at camp. Hopefully they will for you too. But they don't go away for everyone, and we have quite a few fresh faces here that I don't recognize, so I expect nighttime to be pretty loud this year."

Ale sighed as the counselor wearing the name tag that read *NICK* with another eagle silhouette stood on top of a wooden tree stump surrounding the firepit.

"Attention, campers!" he yelled, then blew into the whistle hanging around his neck from a red lanyard, silencing the crowd. Once he received their attention, he continued. "Welcome to Camp Safe Woods!" He held his arms up high as if expecting applause that didn't follow. "Whether you've been here before or if this is your first time with us, we are all glad to have you here. My name is Nick, and I am the head counselor this year. These seven here"—he gestured to those surrounding him—"are the other counselors. If you need anything, please come up to one of us and let us know. Whether you need someone to talk to, you have a question about an activity we're doing, or you just need to know where the bathrooms are, any of us can help you. This is a safe place for everyone, and you all need to know that you are welcome and taken care of while you are here, okay?" He watched the crowd while some of them nodded and others whispered to each other.

"I see you're all still carrying your heavy bags and are probably wondering where to put them right about now,"—he paused, drawing more nods from the campers—"so we're going to get this season started by assigning you to your cabins. Our past campers know this by now, and some of you new folks might've noticed the animal silhouettes on the counselors' name tags. We have four cabins here at Camp Safe Woods that are named after an animal, and each cabin has two counselors supervising it. That doesn't mean they'll be sleeping in the cabin with you, but they are directly in charge of keeping you all safe and making sure everyone is engaging in our activities correctly. Once you're assigned to a cabin, please look for the counselor with the corresponding animal on their nametag."

"Can I be in George's cabin, please?" Ale whispered to Hailey, and followed it with a flirty purr.

"So in order for us to assign your cabins, will all the kids aged twelve and below step this way?" Nick asked.

About five kids that Hailey spotted getting on the bus stepped forward.

"Only five, huh?" Nick asked, looking back at Mitch.

"Parents usually drop off the young ones directly," Mitch explained. "I know more signed up, so they'll be here shortly."

"Okay, then. You kids are gonna be staying in the fish cabin," Nick said.

Two young boys looked at each other, excited. Hailey couldn't decide if it was because they were friends or if they just liked fish. Two counselors with fish silhouettes on their name tags, Jenna and Neil, both stepped forward and introduced themselves to their new charges.

"Campers, Jenna and Neil will show you guys where the fish cabin is. There, you can drop off your bags and they will give you further instructions," Nick said.

Jenna grabbed the hands of the two boys who were excited and began walking away. The other three kids followed them and Neil trailed behind while they all engaged in small talk.

"Now, for the rest of you." Nick picked up a box from behind the stump he stood on. "Inside this box is a bunch of sheets of paper. On each is a picture of one of the animals that represent the cabins. You will come up one by one, quickly grab a piece of paper, and meet with a counselor who has that animal on their name tag. Show them your picture, give them your name, and follow them to the cabin once everyone has chosen from this box. Keep in mind that there is no trading, and you will remain in this cabin for your entire stay here at Camp Safe Woods."

"It sounds like a prison sentence when he puts it like that," Ale said.

"If you don't get a cabin with your friends, congratulations, you will get to make new ones, which is a big portion of your purpose here at camp." Nick stepped down from the stump and held the box out in front of him. "I think that's everything. Come here and pick your animal."

Reminiscent of school bells dismissing a high school class, as soon as he said it, the campers started rushing for the box. "One at a time now," the soft voice of a female camper called out from amongst the madness. Hailey did her best working through the traffic to get to the box, spotting Ale making her choice before she could even see the box over the other campers' heads.

When she finally arrived, she attempted to sneak a peek inside, hoping to catch a glimpse of the animal she would be selecting. Unfortunately, each paper was folded into four squares, concealing the pictures within. Regardless, she wasn't particularly picky about which cabin she ended up in, though George's cabin wouldn't be an awful choice. Ale was more vocal about her preference; she couldn't deny that the man looked good. Taking a chance, she reached into the box and grabbed a piece of paper from the very bottom. Holding onto it tightly, she left the group of campers who were still gathered around Nick and the box. Spotting Ale just outside, she joined her as she walked away from a boy and girl who appeared to be a year younger than them.

"Did you check your paper already?" Ale asked when she spotted Hailey approaching.

"Not yet, you?" Hailey.

"Yeah, I got the bear," Ale said.

"Damn. So no George for you, then," Hailey teased.

"Believe it or not, that couple over there"—Ale pointed to the boy and girl—"wanted to share a cabin. She got the bear, too, but the boy got the squirrel. So we traded." She had a smug expression on her face.

"Didn't that guy say not to trade?"

"It's not like he saw us. All those kids are still surrounding him."

"Wow, lucky you."

"Well, what are you waiting for? Open yours!"

"Oh right!" Hailey held up her paper. She felt her hands surging with a rush of energy as butterflies filled her stomach. Hailey hadn't been this excited since she received her first letter from her imprisoned father. She grabbed one corner of the paper and unfolded it, then unfolded again before turning the page around to show off the squirrel silhouette. The butterflies shot from her stomach and through her body until they escaped through the open smile on her face and all that nervousness became joy. "Yes!"

"Hell yeah! We're roommates!"

"What cabin did you guys get?" a boy asked from behind, interrupting them from jumping up and down with excitement. They both turned and saw Billy holding up his own squirrel silhouette.

"Okay, if we're going to be roommates, you need to promise to stop appearing behind us," Ale said.

"So you got squirrel too?" he asked.

Hailey nodded. "We should probably go meet our counselors."

"You don't need to tell me twice," Ale said, fixing her hair and adjusting her shirt.

They walked toward George and the brunette he stood next to. He was busy entertaining a couple of other campers who approached them first, so the girl turned to them and smiled. "Are you guys squirrels too?"

The three of them nodded and matched her smile, holding up their sheets of paper.

"It's so nice to meet you. I'm Annie."

Chapter 9

"Here we are," Annie said, opening the door to the squirrel cabin and welcoming her campers inside. This cabin was larger than the one she slept in with the other counselors, but it wasn't as inviting. The cabin was rectangular, with six bunk beds facing the center of the room— three on the left and three on the right. There was a long, shaggy rug splitting the floor between them down the center. Beside each bunk bed were small, circular tables on both sides, one for the top bunk and one for the bottom.

Similar to the counselors' cabin, a combined light and fan hung from the ceiling. Directly opposite the entrance was a solitary square window, divided into four small panes by intersecting beams. Below it stood a lengthy dresser resembling the one found in Annie's cabin, featuring empty name tags on each of the drawers, waiting for the campers to claim them at a later time.

The campers hurried inside and quickly started choosing their bunks. Hailey, Ale, and Billy, the three campers

Annie had met first, headed straight to the back of the cabin. Ale tossed her belongings onto the top bunk on the left side, and Hailey claimed the bunk underneath. Billy opted for the bottom bunk across from them on the right.

Her initial impressions of the trio could have been far worse. Until now, Annie had been consumed by worry about caring for children with serious issues. However, these three appeared to be quite ordinary. Ale stood out as a confident and chatty individual, and her humor made Annie quite fond of her. Billy, on the other hand, seemed slightly anxious and eccentric, but he came across as a nice person. As for Hailey, Annie hadn't quite figured her out.

She seemed nice, for the most part, but she said little of anything to convince Annie otherwise. She had the air of someone who always had words on the tip of her tongue, yet opted to remain silent. It was as if shyness held her back from expressing herself, or perhaps she believed her thoughts weren't worthy of being voiced. Regardless, Annie made it a priority this summer to help Hailey loosen up, to see her vibrant and carefree.

"Okay, make yourselves at home but don't get too comfortable, okay? They told us Betty is preparing a very special barbecue to celebrate everyone's arrival," Annie said.

"Thank God, I'm starving," Ale said. The other campers smiled and cheered.

"Before you guys get too excited," George chimed in, "we've got a bit of bad news." The crowd quieted to listen.

"If you've attended camp before, you know this rule by now: before we can get this summer started, we have to collect all of your cell phones.

"Seriously?" Ale asked, surprised. Billy looked at her and nodded, pulling his phone from his pocket. Hailey didn't say much, but her face looked as though she was over the whole camp experience already.

A boy that Annie hadn't met yet raised his hand for a question, but George only continued. "And please don't use those lame 'I don't have a cell phone' or 'I didn't bring my phone to camp' excuses." The boy put his hand down. "People try that every year and it never works. After the kinds of things we've all been through, none of us would leave home without a phone."

"Exactly!" Ale yelled as if she had an epiphany. "If we wouldn't feel safe, why would the camp want to take that comfort away from us?"

"Because my grand—" Annie caught herself. "Because Mitch thinks this would be the best opportunity to teach you guys that we can live safely and independently, free of those devices that you've convinced yourself you can't live without."

"Well said," George commended, nodding in agreement.

The campers gave up, each of them pulling their phones from either their pockets or bags and handing them to George, who collected them in a bag he tied off once he received the final one from Hailey. "Thank you," he said to her.

"If we die, it's your fault," Ale joked. George didn't think it was funny.

"Now that that's over, how about some food?" Annie asked.

"They promised me a barbecue," Ale whispered into Hailey's ear. "Not . . . whatever the hell this is."

Hailey chuckled. Everybody at the camp, including the campers, counselors, nurse, cook, and Mitch, stood—or sat in their wheelchair—around the campfire while Nick held up an American flag and Mitch played "The Star-Spangled Banner" via cassette tape in a portable stereo on his lap.

She habitually placed her hand over her heart whenever this song played before a public event. However, something about this particular rendition felt off. Normally, there would be a talented singer or someone symbolizing heroism entrusted with singing their anthem. But today, all they had was this worn-out cassette tape that kept skipping, much to the amusement of those around her. Each skip was followed by Mitch's attempt to fix the stereo, which elicited more laughter from the crowd.

Hailey struggled to hold back her laughter at the absurdity of it all. She composed herself and observed the serious expressions on people's faces, noticing the tears in their eyes. But her urge to burst into laughter resurfaced when Mitch joined in, singing halfway through the song, prompting others to follow suit. Not because Mitch was a terrible singer, which he was, but because Hailey knew he was trying to cover up the sound of the tape skipping.

Once the song ended, the crowd cheered—some for their American pride and some because they felt they had to. Hailey clapped because she was glad it was over.

Ale sarcastically yelled, "America!" over the clapping while Mitch tossed his stereo hard onto the dirt, annoyed with it. Nick planted the flag in the ground.

The clapping quickly died as soon as Mitch cleared his throat. "Okay, let's eat!" he yelled, bringing more cheering as Betty led the counselors into the cafeteria. They returned with platters of meat, and Betty started cooking.

The barbecue had gone on for well over two hours, and Hailey was starting to feel more comfortable.

Betty was great at cooking, so Hailey knew she would eat well over the summer—a concern she hadn't thought of before now. She sat with Ale and Billy, along with their other cabin members, on log benches. Except when Annie or George would try to get to know them better, they mostly engaged in conversation among themselves. This didn't bother her because she got along well with Ale and Billy, and she was happy to be sorted into their cabin.

"Gosh, I am stuffed." Ale put her paper plate on the dirt beside her feet. It held a half-eaten hot dog and remnants of potato salad.

"Me, too," Hailey said. "Does she cook like this all the time?"

Billy nodded and quickly swallowed the burger that filled his mouth. "Every day. I don't know how she does it. Breakfast, lunch, and dinner."

"I'm sure she has the counselors' help," Ale said, looking into the woods.

Hailey didn't know Ale for long, but after the bus ride and the three times she'd dragged her to the bathroom during the few hours they had been eating together, she knew that Ale had to pee again.

"Hey, Hailey—" Ale started.

Hailey interrupted her, "Okay, let's go." Hailey held her empty plate in one hand and offered the other to help Ale up.

"You don't know what I was gonna—"

"Yeah, I do. Come on." Hailey waved her fingers as if to say, "Hurry." Ale grabbed her hand, and she pulled her up.

"We'll be right back," Ale said.

Billy gave a thumbs-up and nodded, his mouth stuffed with a burger once again.

The bathroom was not too far away, just a hundred yards past the tree line from the camp's main circle. George had explained that it had to be a distance from the camp to avoid attracting bears with the smells. Hailey understood the reasoning behind it, but she wasn't comfortable with the idea of having to go to the bathroom in the middle of the night and walk through the woods alone. Luckily for her, the members of the squirrel cabin had agreed to implement a buddy system. If someone asked you to accompany them on a bathroom trip, you agreed without asking any questions. However, at this point, Hailey had to break that rule.

"So what the hell is wrong with your bladder?" she asked.

"What? I told you I pee a lot." Ale giggled.

"No, a lot is one thing. This is something else. Are you sure something isn't wrong with you?"

"There are a lot of things wrong with me, but my small bladder isn't one of them."

"Are you sure? Maybe you have a UTI ... Oh, maybe you're pregnant!" Hailey joked, and Ale playfully pushed her.

"I'm not fucking pregnant. I would have to at least touch a penis first, and that is not on my agenda." They approached the bathroom. It was a small log building, much like their cabins.

"No?" Hailey stepped up the three stairs and held the door open for her.

Ale looked at her sarcastically before stepping inside. "No." She walked to a stall and locked herself inside while Hailey waited at the door, looking outside and watching the leaves blow in the wind. A beautiful sight until Ale's audibly loud urine stream interrupted it.

"If you're looking to fill a spot on your agenda, I'm sure Billy would be open to it this summer," Hailey said, trying to drown out the sound.

"Ew, are you serious?"

"He seems nice."

"Yeah, sure. But his eyes are on you, girl."

Hailey tilted her head. "What?"

"Don't tell me you haven't noticed him staring at you."

Hailey thought about it but couldn't think of any-thing she had said that was more than friendly. Then her thoughts trailed to the fact that Ale was still urinating. "Okay, pregnant or not, I'm monitoring your fluid intake from now on. That is not normal."

Ale laughed as she finished up. Hailey waited for her to pull up her pants and leave the stall, then she continued to hold the door for her and they started their walk back to camp.

"So I couldn't help but notice you changed the subject when I suggested Billy has a thing for you," Ale said, jumping in front of Hailey and walking backward to keep the pace while looking into her eyes for any nervous tells.

"Did not," Hailey said, trying not to smile. But not so much because she felt nervous, more so because Ale was watching her so intently.

Ale pointed at her, saying, "Yes, you did! You already said, 'He seems nice.' Do you think he seems cute too?"

"I mean, yeah, he's cute but . . . in a dorky—"

Ale interrupted her when she tripped over something and yelped, pulling Hailey's arm as they fell backward into the dirt.

Hailey screamed, "Shit!" in shock, as the fall surprised her.

While Ale screamed, "Fuck!" with distinct pain in her voice.

"What the hell happened?" Hailey looked at Ale, who was completely still, tilting her head so she could see her leg; Ale had tripped over a bear trap that hadn't yet triggered. However, her leg was resting gently on top of its teeth, with cuts across her shin and calf.

"What do I do?" Ale whispered, her voice calm, though her chest heaved with each breath.

"Okay, just be calm. You need to lift your leg up and away quickly. Careful not to press the pressure plate in the center," Hailey said.

"I'm scared."

"I know, but that thing can go off at any second. You need to pull away carefully. Let's do it on three, okay?"

Ale swallowed and nodded. "Okay."

Hailey counted, "One, two, three," and Ale pulled her leg away, shrieking a high-pitched scream in anticipation of her calf muscle getting clamped, but she got away unscathed. She crawled backward and away from the trap toward Hailey, who grabbed her and held her for comfort while Annie and George ran to them from the camp.

"We heard screaming," Annie said.

"Is everyone okay?" George asked, stepping awfully close to the trap.

"Stop!" Both Ale and Hailey yelled at them, holding their hands up like traffic directors.

The counselors stopped in place and waited for further instructions while they both noticed Ale's leg.

"There's a bear trap right there." Hailey pointed to it.

"Oh my God," Annie said.

"What the fuck?!" George exclaimed.

"Did it get your leg?" Annie asked and approached her, lifting her limb so she could get a better look.

"I tripped on it, and the teeth cut up my leg."

"She's lucky it didn't trigger," Hailey said.

"I'll say!" Annie agreed.

George picked up a stick from the ground as Nick ran over.

"Is everyone okay?" Nick asked, as George pressed the stick into the pressure plate of the bear trap, triggering it. They all watched as it clamped down, its teeth crushing the stick and breaking it into pieces. "Is that a fucking bear trap?"

"Alejandra tripped on it, but it didn't go off," Annie explained.

Nick looked confused at first, then looked at Ale and his face changed to concerned, as if his brain took a second to register who Alejandra was.

"Why would there be a bear trap out here in the first place?" Hailey asked.

"There must've been a hunter that left it," George said.

"Doubtful. I'm pretty sure those are super illegal in California. You know, animal rights and all."

"So who left it?" Ale asked.

"That doesn't matter. We need to take you to see Nurse Cherie," Annie said, helping Ale off the ground with Hailey. "Can you walk?"

Ale planted her foot on the ground and tried to stand on her own, but she winced. "It hurts to put pressure on it. I think it's bruised pretty badly."

"Here, let me help you." Hailey grabbed Ale's arm and pulled it over her shoulder to support her, and Annie did the same with her other arm. George returned to the barbecue to make sure their cabin's campers were okay, and Nick led the way through the cafeteria to the nurse's office.

When they opened the door, Cherie was sipping what Hailey assumed was coffee, and she seemed shocked that they entered the room so abruptly. She snorted some of her drink and quickly put it down before jumping to Ale's aid and offering her a seat. "Oh my goodness. What happened?"

The dog Hailey had just seen for the first time earlier today got up from his bed to see what the commotion was about.

"Woodsby, down," Nurse Cherie said, and the dog lay back down.

"She fell over a bear trap," Annie said, helping lower Ale into the chair.

"She what?"

"It didn't trigger, but the teeth fucked my leg up." Ale noticed Nick was watching over her and pretended to care. "Oh, excuse my language."

"You're not wrong," Nick said.

"Yeah, this leg looks bad," Nurse Cherie confirmed, crouching and holding the leg for a better look. "Would you mind if I take your shoe off to do a thorough assessment?"

Ale shook her head. "I don't mind."

Cherie untied the laces of Ale's red Vans shoe and re-moved it, followed by taking off her sock. Her ankle ap-peared more injured than her calf, displaying deep bruising that encircled her Achilles tendon.

"Ouch," Cherie said.

Ale looked away with her fingers covering her eyes. "How does it look? Is it that bad?"

"It's . . . not great," Hailey answered.

"You'll definitely feel it in the morning," Annie said.

Ale caved and looked, curling her upper lip at the sight of it. She muttered, "Fuck" under her breath and shot a quick glance toward Nick, still partially worried that she'd get in trouble. Hailey thought she was possibly testing her limits with the counselors, breaking the seal. "Do I need to . . . like, go to the hospital?"

"No, the hospital shouldn't be necessary. But I have good and bad news." Cherie lowered Ale's foot to the wooden floor. "Bad news is, I have to clean up your cuts, get the dirt out of them, and disinfect them. It's probably going to hurt a lot. Then I'm gonna wrap your leg quite tightly and instruct you to keep it on ice overnight until it's numb, which might be uncomfortable."

"And the good news?" Ale asked.

"You get to hang out with Woodsby and me for the next fifteen minutes while I fix you up." Cherie reached over to pet Woodsby on the head. He didn't bother to wake up.

"Ooh, can I stay?" Hailey asked, coming off a tad more excited than she intended. They all looked at her, awaiting an explanation. "What? I want to pet the dog."

Chapter 10

Hours later, everybody at camp sat around the firepit and watched the embers dance before them. Annie positioned herself next to George near the campers of the squirrel cabin, distributing marshmallows and skewers to everyone. However, due to the large number of people gathered around the firepit, they had to take turns roasting. They decided to let Ale go first, given her injury. Unfortunately, she had to sit in an uncomfortable position, elevating her leg to ice her ankle, which made it difficult for her to reach the fire. Billy kindly offered to hold her skewer alongside his own while he took his turn roasting marshmallows with Hailey.

Mitch cleared his throat to quiet the campers—which Annie realized he did quite often—and the camp went silent, minus the crackling of the fire.

"Good evening, campers! It is my very special honor to welcome you all to our first campfire of the year," he said, followed by clapping from the crowd. "I hope you all enjoyed your first day here at Camp Safe Woods,"—his voice quieted—"minus the one obvious mishap." He looked at Ale and scratched the back of his neck. "Yeah, I should probably talk about that. I'm sure some of you are probably worried after you heard what happened to poor Miss Alejandra." The crowd murmured amongst themselves; some kids asking what happened and others voicing their concerns.

"But let me assure you that it was nothing more than an unfortunate onetime event. With the help of our head counselor, Nick, and our other counselors, Jordan, Jenna, and George, we have scouted the surrounding woods and confirmed that there are no other such traps lying around. We're not sure where it came from, but someone obviously left it to catch an animal and forgot about it." He looked at Ale once again. "And look at that. She's still here, and she is doing fine. Can we all give her a round of applause for her toughness?" Mitch started with a slow clap, and Annie, along with George, Hailey, and Billy, led the way with loud and over-the-top clapping that the rest of the camp followed, erupting into the night with an audible excitement.

Ale tried to hide her smile with her sarcastic eyes, but Annie could tell by the rosiness of her cheeks that she enjoyed the attention.

"Now as some of you may know already, these nightly campfires are very special to us at Camp Safe Woods—and yes, I said, nightly." Mitch settled at his place by the fire and started prepping his marshmallow on a skewer as he continued. "We do these every night because, well, roasting marshmallows is awesome and because we want to give you an enjoyable way to socially gather and tell your stories. And I know you all have a story to tell. Without nightly opportunities, we'd never get through them all!"

He quieted his voice but kept the bass loud enough for them all to hear. Annie knew this was his serious voice. "For you new campers who may be unsure of what I'm talking about, let me elaborate. Everyone at this camp is here because of something dark and tragic that you've been through. Our goal is, to put it lightly, to help you get over it. And by that, I don't mean help you forget about it or act like it never happened. What I mean is, to get you to a place in your life where that dark memory no longer controls you. Where you can sleep at night and have happy dreams again. Where you can think about the faces of those you've lost without crying and remember the good times you've had with them. Where you can go through daily life without seeing small things that trigger your memory and bring back that dreaded feeling of those times when your life was at its lowest point. And I know it won't happen overnight for everybody, but I want to at least show you that this is something we can do for you." Mitch looked down at his marshmallow and it was ablaze, burning black at its tip and dripping white goop from its base. He sighed and threw it into the flame.

"Can I get a show of hands from all of you who can say that this camp helped you achieve this goal?" Mitch asked.

Annie watched about fifty percent of the campers raise their hands, along with all the other counselors minus herself and Nick, who looked as though he was counting the raised hands while nodding.

"Now before you lower your hands, can I get those who might not be there just yet, but feel as though this camp is pushing you in the right direction, to raise their hands as well?" Mitch asked.

Another thirty percent of those around them put their hands up, leaving behind Ale and Hailey, along with those who Annie could only assume were new campers this year.

"Thank you. You can put your hands down," Mitch said. "As you can see, this place is helping those around you who have all gone through something similar. You are not alone in this, and you will get through it. And a big piece of taking your tragic past and refusing to let it control your life is having the ability to tell that story to others. Telling your story can help you understand what happened as best as you can and help you move on. Of course talking about things such as this might sound like an impossible task, but I've heard plenty of these stories from hundreds of campers over the years, and I promise you can do it. Whether you can tell it here, in front of everyone, or to your fellow cabin mates, your counselors, or even just to yourself in the mirror, you will be able to tell that story by the time you leave this camp, and we will all be eager to listen. And to prove it to you, I will now give the platform to any of my counselors who might volunteer to share their story with all of you."

"I'll do it," Jordan said, placing her hands on her knees and rising to her feet.

Mitch nodded. "Thank you."

She waved to the campers. "Hey, everyone. If you don't know by now, my name is Jordan, and I'm a counselor here at Camp Safe Woods. I started attending this camp when I was, like, thirteen years old, even though, unlike most of you, my mom didn't think it was a great idea. Just like the rest of you, I've been through something quite traumatizing, and it actually happened at a summer camp much like this one. The only actual difference was, at that camp, witnessing mass murders wasn't really a prerequisite. It was more of a side effect or bonus feature." She looked around the campsite, expecting laughs, but aside from a few giggles, she mostly received shocked and horrified expressions.

Mitch pinched the bridge of his nose and shook his head in disappointment.

"Oh right," she said. "I'm sorry. I've become desensitized to the idea of death over the years and sometimes forget that what I say might be offensive. But joking about the things that happened to me helps me cope with it, and it might be an excellent tactic for some of you as well. Right, Mitch?"

"I wouldn't say it's an 'excellent tactic.' More like"—Mitch thought about it for a moment—"not the most healthy one. But hey, anything that helps, I guess. Please, continue."

"Okay, so I guess the story starts when my father died. I was really young, and he was my world." She sat back down. "His death hit me very hard and my mom didn't know how to handle me. I was acting out in school, I didn't have any friends, and we were fighting a lot. It wasn't pretty. My mom's response was to send me away to a summer camp." She sniffled and scratched at her nose. "Looking back, it wasn't a terrible idea. She wanted me to go meet new people while getting me out of the house so we wouldn't rip each other's heads off. I can't blame her at all for what I saw while I was there, but I sure did right after it happened."

She took a deep breath. "So, camp was terrible. And not just because I failed to make friends while I was there, but because this was actually a bad summer camp. The owner didn't care much about the place, and the counselors there cared even less. This place was dirty, unsupervised, and uneventful—at least, until the accident happened. About three weeks into camp, the counselors completely quit watching over us and let the campers do whatever we wanted. On this particular day, it was so hot out that we all spent our time at the lake nearby. None of the counselors wanted to do their job, of course, so they drew straws to settle on two counselors, a male and a female, to act as the lifeguards while we were out playing. The others left camp to find a nearby bar, sneak in, and get drunk."

Jordan stood up again and paced around the fire while she continued. "At the lake, the other campers were being rambunctious. Yelling, wrestling, splashing . . . you name it. It wasn't really my vibe, so I just sat off to the side, listening to one of my dad's old CDs and enjoying the sun." She cracked a smile at the thought, then shifted back to her gloomy mood. "There was a boy there named Mark. I don't remember him too well, only that he mostly kept to himself, and that's exactly what he was doing there at the lake. He sat on the edge of the dock, kicking his legs in the water, when a group of four other campers came from behind him, lifted him up with each camper in charge of holding one limb, and threw him in the water. It was only a joke, I'm sure of it. He'd never hurt anybody, and I'd never heard someone say anything bad about him, but those kids just thought it was so funny to throw him in. I remember how loud they were, all laughing when they did it."

She looked up at the moon for a few seconds before continuing.

"What they didn't realize was that he flailed in the air and smacked his head on one of the dock pilings on the way down. It knocked him unconscious immediately upon impact. When one kid pointed out that Mark hadn't floated back up to the surface, the laughing finally ceased. They questioned where the hell he was and whether or not he knew how to swim. They freaked out, calling to the lifeguards for help, but they weren't there. As it turned out, putting hormonal teenagers in tight red swimsuits led to some"—she looked at the crowd and realized the young ages of some campers—"degenerate actions." She held one hand against the side of her mouth, hiding the letters she spelled out, "S-E-X."

"We got that," Nick said.

"Great." She gave him a thumbs-up. "So, to the surprise of all of us, Mark was actually the son of the camp's owner, Ron. And Ron made some miracle decision that day to show up at camp and check on its operation for the first time that year. While he couldn't find any counselors who were supposed to be running the place, he found his son's corpse as it washed ashore. The campers apologized and pointed fingers at each other, but he didn't care—about anything. He stood there, silent, with an expressionless face until he simply walked away. We didn't see him again until later that night, after the counselors had returned from the bar and reported what happened to Mark to the police. They sat us around a campfire and scolded us for bullying, but we could all tell they were afraid because every one of them knew this was their fault in one way or another. That lecture felt like it was going to go on forever until the bolt from a crossbow pierced the skull of the speaking counselor's skull and emerged from her right eyeball.

"Luckily, that was the only murder I witnessed. As soon as it happened, everybody scattered. I ran straight to my cabin and hid under the bed after putting on my headphones and listening to my dad's CD once again. Hearing the music he used to play around me made me feel safe—like he was there with me, protecting me. I closed my eyes and lay there for hours, only opening them to restart the CD after it finished. When I thought it was safe, I came out from under the bed and tried looking for help. The camp was silent and seemingly abandoned. The only people I found were the corpses of the counselors Ron got ahold of, including the two counselors-slash-lifeguards who were responsible for watching his son. Rumor has it, he found them having sex *again* that night and killed them during the act."

She looked around at the horrified campers before continuing.

"And when the police showed up, right when I felt I was the safest, Ron appeared from the darkness and"—she lifted her shirt, exposing her belly and a long scar around the right side of her abdomen—"he stabbed me. Luckily, the cops had good aim because they shot him before he could stab me again. And I'm even more lucky because they drove fast to the hospital, so I didn't bleed out in their—"

"Okay," Mitch interrupted. "I think we got the gist."

"Sorry, was that too graphic?" Jordan asked.

Mitch held his index and thumb close together, indicating "just a little bit." Annie noticed some kids around the fire looked clearly uncomfortable.

"I'm sorry, guys. Like I said, I'm a bit too desensitized to this whole thing. But being comfortable telling your story is what we're trying to achieve here, so I hope you can at least take that much from me." Jordan smiled.

"Thank you, Jordan," Mitch said. "If anybody else wants to share, we're all ears here." He looked around the fire for any volunteers. When nobody raised their hand, he turned to Ale. "Alejandra! Ale, how about we give you the floor first since you were injured?"

"And follow a story as good as hers? No, thanks. I'm afraid I don't really have one to tell," she said.

"Nonsense," Mitch countered.

"It's okay. "It's getting late. I'm sure everybody is tired from traveling today. It might be best to get the campers to bed soon," Nick suggested.

Mitch looked disappointed, but he agreed. "Good idea. That's why you're the head counselor. If you haven't had a turn at the fire yet, make sure you get at least one marshmallow roasted. We'll be putting the fire out in twenty minutes, then you need to find your cabin's counselors and follow them to your cabin. We will do this again to-morrow, and I look forward to hearing the rest of your stories."

Following a quick trip to the nurse's office to have Ale's bandages changed and spending some time with Park Ranger Woodsby, the girls returned to their cabin equipped with a pair of crutches that Cherie found while going through a storage closet. As soon as they entered the cabin, the other campers inside hurried to Ale's side, bombarding her with questions.

"Are you okay?"

"Did it hurt?"

"Do you think the trap was there on purpose?"

"Is there anything I can do to help?"

Ale only had the energy to respond to that last one. "I just need to get to bed," she said, waving them off, squeezing between them, and even forcing one guy out of her way with a crutch.

Hailey followed carefully behind her to their shared bunk bed and watched Ale stare blankly at the ladder she would have to ascend.

"Sorry, Hailey, but I think we're gonna have to switch beds," Ale said.

"Yeah, of course," Hailey agreed, already removing her things off the bottom bunk. She also brought Ale's stuff down, then held her hand as she lowered into bed.

"Thank you," she said, bundling a blanket at the foot of the bed to elevate her ankle.

"You're welcome. Do you need anything else?" Hailey waited with one foot planted on the bottom step of the ladder.

"I'll be okay," Ale said, sorting through one of her bags.

Hailey climbed the ladder and settled herself on the bed. She pulled her stuffie, Lana, close to her and rummaged through her bag, searching for something more comfortable to sleep in. As she did so, she noticed the sound of rustling coming from the bed opposite theirs. Billy, shirtless and tucked under his blanket, sat up.

"How are you doing?" he asked Ale.

"It's not that bad, really," she said.

"Crazy for a first day at camp, huh?"

"Is it always this eventful?"

Billy laughed. "Nope. Not until you got here."

"Figures." She giggled.

"Injuries aside, did you have fun at least?"

"Uh"—she paused for a moment as if considering the question—"yeah, I think I did." She waited another moment before continuing. "It'll be an interesting summer."

"What about you, Hailey?"

"Huh?" Hailey asked, pretending as though she wasn't eavesdropping on their conversation.

"What do you think of the place?" Ale asked on Billy's behalf, leaning her head out from under Hailey's bunk to see her.

"Oh! It's nice, I think." Hailey picked out a matching red flannel pajama set and placed them on the bed before zipping up her bag. "I have to admit, with the stuff I've gone through"—she looked at Lana for reassurance—"I didn't think a place like this could do anything for me. But after hearing that counselor's story and seeing how comfortable she was telling it, I'm thinking my story isn't so unique, and this place might actually be qualified." She tossed aside her blanket and descended the ladder.

"Does that mean you're ready to tell me your story?" Ale joked and placed her bags on the floor beside the bed. She had her own sleep clothes folded neatly by her elevated ankle.

Hailey took a seat on the edge of her bed and laughed. "Maybe I'll tell you my story when you can stand on your own two feet again."

"You're such a bitch. I bet it's not as crazy as the shit that girl went through. I mean, Jesus Christ, did you hear that? Those kids just drowned that little boy when they barely even knew him. And don't get me wrong, I'd want to hold everybody at fault accountable, too, but slaughtering them like that? I can't imagine the fear those campers felt."

"I can," Billy said, making the conversation even more depressing.

"Same," Hailey said. "I even felt it myself."

Ale's eyebrows raised—half shocked, half uncomfortable.

"You ready to walk to the bathroom?" Hailey asked, lifting the pajamas she held and placing a hand on Ale's knee.

Her eyebrows dropped to normal, and she smiled. "Yeah, let's go."

Chapter 11

"Are you guys not seeing the problem here?" Max asked, lying on his bed beneath the blankets.

"I just don't think it's that serious," George said, changing his shirt.

"It isn't," Vera agreed.

"Come on!" Max sat up in disbelief. "You're joking, right? Jordan, back me up here."

"Don't look at me."

"You're telling me a fucking bear trap at the camp doesn't set off any of your slasher red flags?"

"Is the bear trap really what you're worried about?" Vera asked, and Annie felt a sudden shift of mood in the room.

Max raised an eyebrow. "What?"

"You know what I mean."

He shook his head. "Can't say that I do."

"Dude, you've been worried about Casey since you got here," George said.

"Yeah, but I don't see how that's—"

"This bear trap fiasco clearly gave you more of a reason to worry—" Vera said, interrupted by a single loud snore from Neil in the back of the room. The counselors paused for a moment, looking at him in silence, before continuing their conversation.

"That's not true! This is a big deal. That poor girl could've lost her foot," Max said.

"And now you're worried that Casey has her foot caught in a trap in the middle of the woods, screaming for help, starving and alone," Jordan said, emphasizing her statement with a resistance-filled tug of a bite from her Red Vines licorice. "I don't blame you for freaking out. It's a scary thought."

"See? Jordan agrees with me!"

"Don't get ahead of yourself," she said. "I said I don't blame you for freaking out. I didn't say anything about agreeing. You're definitely worried too much. We all know how loud a mouth Casey has, and that's coming from her best friend. If she got lost in the woods somewhere, someone would definitely hear her screaming.

"Unless she's dead," Max said. Annie was sure this would make the vibe in the room even worse, but it didn't seem to faze anybody.

"And you guys say *I* watch too many scary movies," Jordan said.

"Look, nobody's dead, and nobody's losing any feet. Not while I'm in charge, at least," Nick said.

"'Not while I'm in charge,'" Max said in a mocking voice. "Who do you think you are, fucking Superman?"

"Damn, dude, chill," George said.

Max's shoulders fell as he exhaled. "You're right. Sorry, Nick. This whole thing just doesn't feel right to me."

"Don't worry about it."

"Look, Max, we get it," George assured.

"We all get it," Jordan repeated, waving her arm around the room to include the other counselors. "Okay, sure. The bear trap is a bit of a red flag, but we looked around and didn't find any others. We don't know where it came from, and there was just one. As for Casey,"—Jordan grabbed her clothes and put her bag down—"she's just ghosting you. I hate to say it, and I'm sorry. But it's the truth."

"No . . . She wouldn't. And who are you to say what is and isn't the truth?" Max questioned.

Jordan turned to him with the look of a doctor who brings a terminal diagnosis to a patient. "I'm her best friend, and we tell each other things."

Max just watched as she left the cabin for the shower.

"Hey, I'm sor—" Jenna stepped to him, her hand out and ready to be placed on his shoulder.

"Don't!" Max interrupted, pushing her hand away. He clenched his teeth. "Sorry, Jenna, I just . . . Has she been talking to Casey this whole time? Did she really know about this and just let me worry?" He looked at the other counselors and they all either shrugged their shoulders or shook their heads, except for Neil, who continued to snore.

"I don't know." Jenna started, putting her hand on Max's shoulder this time and taking a seat beside him on the bed, "but we'll talk to her, okay?" She looked at Annie, who nodded her head.

"Yeah, we will," Annie agreed.

"Okay, thank you," he said.

Jenna hugged him and when she pulled away, she booped him on the nose. "No more worrying about the bear trap. Deal?"

He nodded. Jenna stood from the bed, and he lay down to stare at the ceiling. Annie and the gals grabbed their sleep clothes and hurried to catch Jordan at the showers.

As she opened the door to the shower room, Vera yelled, "Jordan, are you in here?" Her voice had to compete with the sound of the shower water splashing against the floor, and she noticed the clothes Jordan had worn all day piled on the floor in front of the only shower stall with a closed curtain.

Annie twisted the dial on the light timer, ensuring they had a full sixty minutes. Following Jenna's lead, she made her way to the counter, placing her neatly folded clothes on its surface. Meanwhile, Vera's heavy footsteps resonated as she stomped toward Jordan's shower. With a forceful pull, she yanked back the shower curtain just as the water abruptly ceased pouring. Annie's eyes involuntarily glanced toward the commotion, catching a glimpse of a frustrated and completely naked Jordan. In a swift motion, she averted her gaze and refocused her attention on the counter. As Annie and Jenna shed their own clothes, a mix of anticipation and nervous energy filled the room.

"Jesus Christ, Vera!" Jordan pulled the curtain shut and yanked the shower chain. "Haven't you heard of privacy?"

"You didn't answer me! I was just making sure you were okay." Vera joined them at the counter and began undressing.

"Why wouldn't I be?"

"I don't know! Bear trap, maybe?" Vera stripped out of her clothes and stepped into a stall.

"In the shower?"

Jenna hopped into a stall, and Annie did the same, pulling the chain for the water as soon as she stepped in. Her spine shivered as the water enveloped her; she had forgotten just how cold the water was.

"You've seen more slasher movies than any of us. You should know all the terrors that happen when girls are in the shower, right?" Vera joked.

"I do, and none of them involve a fucking bear trap. But that would be really cool . . ." Jordan said, trailing off at the end like she was making a mental note. "But, still. Boundaries, Vera."

"Yeah, whatever. Can we talk about what's going on with Casey and Max?"

"What about it?"

"Did you mean what you said?" Annie asked. "About the ghosting?"

"Of course I did."

"But how do you know that? Did she actually tell you?" Jenna probed.

"Yeah, she did." Jordan paused. "Well, not exactly."

"What does that even mean?" Vera asked.

"She didn't exactly say she was going to ghost Max, but about a month ago, she told me she planned to break things off with him. She's moving across the country for college next semester and knew that Max would try to make their relationship more official this summer. That would only complicate things for her because she would feel obligated to say yes, and she wasn't sure if she could handle a long-distance relationship. Plus, you know she has trust issues after what happened to her. She has trouble letting people get that close," Jordan explained.

"So how does that equate to ghosting?" Jenna asked.

"Knowing her, she probably couldn't handle the idea of letting him go and thought this would be the only way she could do it."

"So . . . in reality, you don't know if she ghosted him or not," Vera said.

Jordan paused, the silence exaggerated because Jenna and Annie's water had cut out at the same time.

"Sure, but what else was I gonna tell him? If I didn't say something to calm him down, we'd have to hear about it all summer."

"Yeah, but you might've come off a little strong. Now instead of worried, he's upset," Annie said.

Jordan sighed. "I know, and I'm worried too. I'm just better at hiding it. And if all of us counselors are worried, we won't be any help to the campers, will we?"

"Really? What do you have to be worried about?" Vera asked.

Another pause from Jordan before she answered, "Can I tell you guys something and have you keep it a secret?"

"It depends," Vera said.

"Of course we will," Jenna assured. "Right, Vera?"

"No promises. What if I need to blackmail her in the future?"

Jenna sighed. "What is it, Jordan?"

"I have the key," she answered.

"What key?" Vera asked.

"The key for the storage cabinet that our phones are stored in. I'm the one Nick gave the key to. And I've been sneaking into that room to use my phone whenever I can, trying to get a hold of Casey, but she still hasn't responded to any of my texts. To make matters worse, I've tried calling her, and I get sent straight to voicemail . . . like her phone has been off for days."

"And that's why you're worried?" Jenna asked.

"Partially. What really worries me is that I called her dad and asked him if Casey was still coming to camp, and he said she'd already left."

"So she is coming?" Vera asked.

"If she was, she would've been here by now," Jenna said.

"It sounds bad, right?"

"Yeah, like, really bad," Vera agreed.

"Should we tell someone? This sounds like something we should report," Jenna suggested.

"No, no. I don't want to worry her dad if Casey ends up being okay. I don't think he could handle the thought of losing another kid."

"We should at least talk to Mitch about it," Annie said.

"Just give me tomorrow. I'll try calling her again, and if she doesn't answer, I'll talk to her dad."

"Okay, but . . . can I check my phone?" Vera asked.

"Seriously?!" Jenna exclaimed.

"Yeah! Why not?"

"Because there are more important things to worry about right now."

"Who's worrying? Jordan said it herself, we won't be any help to the campers if we're all worried."

"You won't be any help if you're on your phone either. Besides, if you get caught, I'll get in trouble. Sorry, but no."

"Not fair," Vera said. They could all hear her pouting through her voice.

Annie's water stopped once again, this time without Jenna's following suit. "I feel like my water stops running faster every time," she said, pouring shampoo into her hands and running them through her hair.

"You never really get used to it," Vera said as her water stopped and she pulled her curtain open.

"Are you done already?" Annie finished lathering her hair, pulled the chain, and tilted her head up to the faucet, anticipating cold water to splash her face, only it didn't come.

"Yeah, the quicker I get out of the cold, the better," Vera answered.

Annie opened one eye carefully—just in case the water came down all at once—and pulled the chain again. Still nothing. "What the hell?"

"Is everything okay?" Jenna asked.

"I'm not getting any water!" She pulled the chain multiple times and nothing happened.

"Really?" Vera asked before opening Annie's curtain, scaring her.

"Jesus!" Annie scurried to cover herself with her arms and hands as best as she could. Vera, already wrapped in a towel, looked past her and grabbed the chain, pulling it herself as if Annie wasn't doing it right. "What did Jordan say about boundaries?"

"Hmm? I don't remember. But something's wrong with your shower. Just use mine," Vera said and left the stall, leaving the curtain wide open.

Annie stood there briefly with her jaw agape in disbelief at Vera's comfort level. Then she grabbed her conditioner with one hand and awkwardly covered her pubic region with the other while she hurried into Vera's stall. "I swear I can never shower in peace at this camp," she said.

"Sounds like something out of a slasher." Jordan snickered.

"Ha ha, very funny," Annie said, pulling the shower chain. No water came out. "You're joking, right?"

"What now?" Jordan asked.

"This one doesn't have any water either," Annie whined, instinctively covering herself up in case Vera wanted to walk in and check again, but she didn't.

"Quit breaking all the showers, please. We need to make sure they work before the boys wake up.

"It's not like I'm doing it on purpose!"

"It shouldn't be a big problem. These showers are always finicky," Jenna said.

"How about you just use mine? The water's still running." Jordan offered.

"You mean, join you?" Annie asked.

"What? No. Having Vera practically jump in here with me was already too much. I'm getting out now anyway."

"Okay, thank you," Annie said, peeking her head out of the stall and watching Jordan step out and wrap herself in a towel just as Vera dropped hers to put her underwear on.

"Whatever you do, make it quick. I am freezing my tits off out here!" Vera exclaimed.

"Then put a fucking shirt on," Jordan said.

Annie stepped out of her stall and tiptoed to Jordan's. Hurrying to close the curtain behind herself, she slipped on the soapy floor. As she fell, she gripped the curtain and pulled it down with her, ripping the curtain rod from the wall. It made a loud clang as it bounced on the floor. Vera and Jordan ran to her, and Jenna stepped out of her stall to make sure she was okay, but all she felt was a slight bruising on her ass and some extreme embarrassment that was only slightly assuaged by the fact that they were all seeing each other naked that night. She said the only thing that came to mind, "Ouch."

Vera stepped over the curtain with a teasing smile, her fingers grabbed the chain and gave it a playful tug. Cold water cascaded down directly onto Annie. "At least the shower works."

Chapter 12

Despite her familiarity with long nights, Hailey's first night at camp felt like the longest of her life. Between Ale's agonizing moans, the unknown roommate's night terror, her own nightmares, and helping Ale navigate through the woods to the bathroom on two occasions, Hailey found it challenging to get even two consecutive hours of sleep. And then she was abruptly awakened by the sound of a bell ringing outside.

"What the hell is that?" Ale asked. The cabin filled with the rustling sounds of campers pushing their blankets aside.

"That means it's time to get up," Billy said.

"Are you serious?" Ale sneered.

"Why can't we just sleep?" Hailey asked.

"They only use those bells when they actually have something planned for the day. Unfortunately, that means we've got at least a week's worth of early mornings," Billy said. "If I remember correctly, the first bell means we have an hour to get ready and meet them by the fire."

"What happens if we just want to sleep in?" Hailey asked, rolling over onto her increasingly uncomfortable bed.

"Then the counselors will probably come in and wake you up," Billy said.

"You're telling me George will come in here and lift me out of bed? Count me in," Ale said.

Hailey smirked. "Nope, you're too fragile. He wouldn't want to hurt you. He'd lift me first, just to set an example."

"Or he'll see me being fragile as all the more reason to help. He might even carry me straight into the shower and scrub me down."

"In your dreams."

"You're damn right,"

"There will be no scrubbing," Billy said. "Besides, if I were you, I would hurry and get to the showers. They give the girls the first thirty minutes to shower before any boys can, and if you miss out, you'll have to wait until later."

"I'll just wait until the showers are empty and see if George will help me," Ale said. Hailey grabbed her pillow, reached down to Ale's bunk, and tossed it at her head. "All right, all right, I'll get up. But if George won't help me, who will?"

"Listen, I'll help you get to the shower. After that, you're on your own," Hailey said and hopped down from her bunk.

"All right, folks," Nick said upon gathering the exhausted counselors in the cafeteria. Annie and the rest sat at the tables while he paced in front of a bulletin board on the wall that Annie was certain wasn't there the day before. "Your campers are getting ready at the moment, so you need to know the plan for the day. We will start every morning in a similar fashion— waking up and meeting here for a quick counselor briefing. Then we will all collect our campers at their respective cabins and meet around the campfire to tell them the day's agenda."

Annie yawned and rubbed her eyes.

"I've taken it upon myself to bring this 'job board' to camp, to make it simple for us to determine where we are all expected to work during the day. This way, I can assign you all to a position before you're awake, and you won't have to ask me repeatedly what your job is." Nick turned and pointed at the board. "Underneath each job title, I have placed an animal's silhouette. That job assignment is expected to be taken on by both counselors of the cabin depicted. As you can see, I've already assigned everybody."

Following Vera, who got up first, the counselors all approached the board to get a better look. The job board had multiple listings—most were empty—and Annie just quickly scanned them to find which ones had animals beneath them. First, beneath the sign for *COOKING*, was the bear silhouette—Max and Jordan's cabin. Then, *DISHWASHING*—Nick and Vera's cabin, the eagle. Near the bottom left of the bulletin board was the sign for *CABIN CLEANING*, and beneath it was Jenna and Neil's fish logo. Last, Annie stared blankly at her squirrel silhouette pinned neatly beneath a sign marked *LIFEGUARD*.

"Dishwashing? You're joking," Vera complained.

"I wish I was, but I'll be doing it too. We only have to wash the dishes from yesterday and this morning's breakfast, though, so if we get it done early enough, we can have the rest of the day off," Nick said. "Maybe even get some time at the lake."

"I'm sorry, but does that say lifeguard?" Annie asked.

"Yeah, it does," Nick confirmed. "Mitch and I thought it would be a great idea to break the campers out of their shell. First full day at camp, send them to the lake for a swim. Assuming they brought swimsuits, of course. Oh! Speaking of which . . ." Nick walked to a nearby table with a box on top of it, picked it up, and dumped the contents onto the table—a large mix of swimsuits, including one-pieces, two-pieces, and men's trunks of varying lengths. There were multiple sizes of each item, all of them bright red with the signature Camp Safe Woods logo.

"Mitch didn't want to offend anybody asking for sizes, but he wanted each of us to have a swimsuit representing our camp. So I guess, go through these and try to find one you like."

"Hell yeah!" Vera said, running to the table and rummaging through the bikini options.

"Cooking?" Max asked. "Don't we have a chef for that?"

"Yeah, but cooking for fifty people isn't a one-person job. It will be your job to assist," Nick said. "And don't think these jobs are permanent. We will rotate every day, so everyone will have to do everything. No room for anyone to be lazy here." He looked at Neil, but he didn't seem to notice, still looking at the board.

"So . . . cabin cleaning," Neil said. "Is that just our cabin, or the campers' cabins too?"

"Every cabin. But lucky for us, it's mostly just dusting and vacuuming and making sure there isn't anything that might attract bears. Don't bother touching anybody's things or making beds. It will be one of the easiest jobs of the summer unless campers sneak food inside or spill stuff. Most of that job will be walking from cabin to cabin."

Neil sighed. "I don't like walking."

"Nobody does," Nick said, then looked at his watch. "Okay, the campers should be done by now. Let's all make sure they're ready and everyone meet by the firepit."

Annie and George selected a few swimsuit options before gathering their campers and leading them to the firepit. Along the way, Alejandra repeatedly requested a piggyback ride, but George kept refusing. They were the second group to arrive, right after the eagle cabin campers, who seemed much sleepier compared to the squirrels. As they waited, Annie and George mingled with their campers. Finally, after the fish cabin arrived, Mitch showed up.

"Good morning, everyone," he said, rolling his wheelchair with the posture of somebody late to a meeting. "I hope you all enjoyed your first night." He looked at Ale as he rolled by her. "Are you doing okay?"

She smiled and nodded.

"I'm going to keep this short and sweet. Betty, along with some helpful counselors, will cook you all a fabulous breakfast to prepare you for the day. Then the counselors of the squirrel cabin will lead you all to the lake for a fun day of swimming. It's supposed to be a hot day, so put on sunscreen. If you don't have any, make sure to talk to Nurse Cherie before you go out there. I expect everyone to get in the water at least once, but you don't have to be out there all day. After a few hours, we will open up the camp for some free time—keeping the lake open, of course. If you wish to leave the lake, meet with one of the lifeguards and sign out."

"If George takes his shirt off, I'll gladly stay at the lake," Ale whispered to Hailey. She looked embarrassed when she noticed Annie heard her, but when Annie laughed, Ale smiled at her.

Mitch thought for a moment before continuing. "Well, I don't really have much else to say. Get a good look at the counselors if you haven't already. Feel free to ask any of them questions or let them know if you need anything. Hmm . . . what else? Nick, do you have anything to add?"

"Nope."

"Alrighty then, I won't hold you any longer. Run on to the cafeteria and enjoy your breakfast, then go back to your cabins and get ready to enjoy some time at the lake."

The sound of campers dispersing from the meeting reminded Annie of when the bell would ring at high school, signaling for lunchtime.

Chapter 13

Cooking breakfast wasn't the most dreadful chore. Betty had already prepared the pancake mix before Max and Jordan arrived in the kitchen, so all Max had to do was pour some on the griddle, keep an eye on them, flip them once, wait a bit, and transfer them onto plates. However, what made the task slightly more unpleasant was Max's feeble attempt to ignore Jordan, who was supposed to fry the bacon. After the conversation they had the previous night about Casey ghosting him, Max was overwhelmed with frustration and denial. Unfortunately, he decided to direct his negative emotions toward Jordan by giving her the cold shoulder.

Naturally, this was hard to do when they were working together. Plus, Jordan wasn't her usual charismatic, quirky self today. She seemed to be either genuinely upset that she said what she did or regretful that it had to be her to tell Max the truth. His problem was that he couldn't decipher what actually went on in her head, and he knew nobody else at camp could either. Jordan's emotions were always hard to read since she was the kind to joke and laugh at her pain, but remain lazy and tucked away on days that she would call better ones. Something just didn't feel right about today.

She wasn't making her usual slasher movie references, she wasn't coming up with any witty jokes, and Max felt as though Jordan had trouble looking at him. Sure, Max's drive to ignore her didn't give her much to go on as far as conversation was concerned, but she was always the talkative one who would break the ice. This time, it looked like there was something she wanted to get off her chest, and Max couldn't tell if it was "I'm sorry about last night" or "I'm sorry I didn't tell you sooner."

Instead, when she did finally speak, all she said was, "I burned this one," picking out a charred strip of bacon from her pan and lowering it into her mouth, following that with a cute squeak and sticking her tongue out after burning it. Max wanted to be so mad at her, but seeing her go from being so glum to so cute in that brief span of time made it hard for him. He laughed at her and she flipped him off, so he stuck his tongue out to mock her, then he looked at his pancakes on the griddle and saw them burning.

Max scrambled for the spatula and flipped them all over, but there was no saving them, so he tossed them and scraped the burnt remains into the corner of the griddle while Jordan laughed behind him. He reached for the bowl of pancake mix and tilted it to pour more, but it was empty. He looked at Jordan, who was watching him with an ice cube held to her tongue when Betty entered through the swinging double doors holding a large black serving tray and folding table.

She placed the tray on the counter beside the plates that Max and Jordan had prepared, then looked at them both before focusing on the ice against Jordan's tongue, then looked at the water on the floor that had dripped off of Jordan's fingertips. "Make sure you clean that up before you leave here. I don't want to slip on it later." Jordan nodded. Betty took the plates from the counter and put them on the serving tray, leaving just two behind, nodding at them as she lifted the tray. "Those two are for you. Don't worry about cleaning any dishes. I'll make sure Nick does it before you two get back here to help with lunch."

"Thanks, Betty," Max said, and she walked out of the kitchen, the double doors swinging back and forth behind her. Once she was gone, Max and Jordan turned off the stove and griddle, then he leaned against the counter by their plates, watching her towel up the water from the floor. "Are you hungry?" he asked, before the oncoming awkward silence could make its appearance.

She looked at him, then at her plate. "Starving." She walked to the counter and tapped her fingers on it as if she had something to say, but she wasn't sure how.

"Is everything okay?"

"Would you want to go somewhere private?" she answered.

"What?" Max asked, confused.

"I mean, you and me. We could take our breakfast somewhere away from the camp and the others," she said, kicking her foot against the floor like she was nervous.

Max wasn't sure what was going on. First, she throws the Casey accusation at him and storms out of the cabin, then she spends the whole morning avoiding him, and now she wants to eat breakfast alone with him. Considering her motives, the only thing that made sense in his mind was that she was flirting with him. "What's this about?" he asked.

"After breakfast, everyone is going to the lake or working, but us. We'll have a few hours where nobody will need us, so I thought we could go somewhere secluded and hang out," she said, looking him in the eyes for the first time today.

"You want to hang out?" Max started feeling nervous. Was she actually coming on to him? He wasn't used to the feeling, so he didn't want to jump to conclusions, but he thought it made sense, given the way she had been acting. If she had developed an infatuation with him, it would explain her nervousness when approaching him. Plus, it would explain why she said what she did about Casey. The thought of her making up something like that to open up Max's availability crossed his mind.

"Yeah, why not? We're gonna hang out a lot, working the same cabin all summer. We might as well break the ice and get a little closer to each other," she said.

Max found himself in a dilemma. He was convinced that she was flirting with him, but he was unsure how to react. If she had fabricated the whole story about Casey ghosting her, he would be filled with anger. But what if she was telling the truth? In that case, his anger should be directed toward Casey for leaving without a word. Max saw himself as a single man facing a girl who presented an opportunity for him to make a move. Moreover, making a move on Jordan, Casey's best friend, seemed like the perfect way to get back at her. If Jordan's claims were accurate and Casey had truly ghosted him, Max would find it difficult to feel remorseful about any actions he took in response.

If things don't work out with Casey, why not give Jordan a try? It might seem a bit hasty since he just found out last night, but he's heard stories about rebounds, and they all seem to involve impulsive decisions with strangers. However, this situation was different because Jordan was far from being a stranger—they practically grew up together and went through similar experiences. She would understand his trauma and know how to handle it, unlike most people. Plus, even though she may not fit the typical "pretty girl" stereotype like Casey, she still looked just as good without putting in as much effort.

Of course there was always the possibility that Max was completely misreading the situation—which he had a tendency of doing with girls—and she might genuinely just want to get more comfortable with him for the sake of work. Considering this, he thought it might be best to follow her lead without further jumping to conclusions.

"It could be fun," she said, impatience appearing in the way her eyebrows rose.

"Okay, sure . . . let's do it." Max grabbed their plates and handed Jordan hers.

"Great. I just need to make a quick stop before we go."

"Bathroom break?"

"No, I just need to grab something from our cabin really quickly."

What would she need to grab to eat breakfast? Max thought, following closely behind her as she left the kitchen.

At the cabin, he held the door for her as she entered and turned on the light. Then he watched from the open doorway as she went to her bed and grabbed her backpack that leaned against the wall.

"What's in there?" he asked.

"A secret." She giggled, walking past him through the door.

He followed her past the showers and deep enough into the woods that they couldn't see any buildings past the trees. He felt a little uncomfortable.

"Where are—"

"This should be fine," she interrupted and gently placed her plate on the ground before sliding her backpack off and dropping it.

"Here?"

"It's as good a place as any," she said, taking a seat on the ground beside a tree and unzipping her bag.

He looked down and didn't like the thought of eating so close to the dirt, but he took a seat anyway, two feet across from her. "So, what's the secret?"

"Here it is," she said, pulling a Ziploc bag from the backpack. "Ta-da!" she exclaimed, presenting the bag to him, and he took it.

Lighter than he thought, he only had a vague idea of the contents of the bag, which he immediately confirmed upon opening it and the smell hit him in the face. The bag was filled to the brim with joints. "What the hell is this?" He held the bag up and examined it like a boy discovering his first pair of women's panties.

"My secret stash." She grabbed the bag and took a joint, putting it between her lips.

"Is this why you brought me all the way out here?"

She nodded as she held the flame to it before tossing the lighter into her open backpack. She took a long inhale and blew the smoke out of the side of her mouth. "Things got a little heated last night. I just wanted to clear the air, and I thought this was the best way to do it."

"By smoking?"

"Exactly. We're both on edge with this whole Casey thing, and our emotions can run pretty high." She pulled the joint from her lips. "This can calm that down enough for us to talk about it." She offered it to him.

"I don't know," he said, reluctant because he'd never smoked before.

"Do it for me?" she teased.

He reached out and took it from her, then dragged it to his mouth. "How do I do it?"

She laughed. "Seriously?"

"Do you want me to or not?"

"Duh."

"Then teach me."

"Just inhale. And hold it, but not too—"

He interrupted her with a coughing fit. The smoke filled his lungs faster than he expected, making him cough uncontrollably until he felt like he could breathe again, then he spit out the drool that filled his mouth while he held the joint out like it was an armed weapon he felt unsafe holding.

She laughed again, taking it from his hand. "At least let me finish telling you how before you do it."

"Good idea," he croaked in his airless voice.

"See, watch me." She held it to her lips and inhaled for just a second and blew it out right after.

"It looked cooler the way I did it," he joked.

"I thought so too." She offered it back to him. "Try again?"

"Yeah." He grabbed it and inhaled, much less than last time, and held it inside until he felt the need for oxygen, then exhaled.

"Much better," she said, reaching for the joint. "Almost like you know what you're doing."

He laughed.

"I like you, you know," she said.

Max looked at her. Was that a confession? Weed doesn't work that fast, does it?

"You're funny. And personally, I thought you were great for Casey, but I didn't really believe in your relationship from the beginning." She passed the joint to him.

"Excuse me?" He took it and inhaled, feeling much more comfortable with it this time around.

"I don't mean that in a bad way. Just that, I knew it wasn't a serious thing like you wanted everyone else to believe."

Max looked at her like he couldn't believe what she was saying.

"You don't have to act like I'm crazy. Casey already told me you guys started the whole 'summer camp boyfriend and girlfriend' thing for the sake of looking cooler than the other campers." Max looked down at the dirt, unable to deny it.

She held her hand out. "Pass it here." He placed it between her fingers. "Don't get me wrong, I'm not judging you at all. I understand why you guys started the whole facade. You were young. But I couldn't understand why you kept it up for so long—at least, until last year."

He looked up, interested in her theory. "And why is that?"

"Because you eventually developed actual feelings and didn't want that relationship to end."

Bingo, he thought. *She hit the nail on the head.* "What makes you say that?"

She looked at him like he was dumb. "I think it's pretty obvious."

"Enlighten me."

"Maybe the way you looked at her? Or how about the way you treated her? You walked around this camp like she was royalty. You always let her go first during activities, you would offer her extra food from your plate at lunchtime, you would somehow end up in her cabin every year and take the bunk just below hers. I mean, really? Do I need to say more? Oh, and don't get me started on the CDs."

"What's wrong with the CDs?"

"Nothing's wrong with them; they are undeniable evidence of your feelings for her. You wanted to give her a piece of you to take home every year to feel closer to her. As a fellow music enthusiast, I can't think of something that spells out, 'I love you' more than that. It's just a shame she didn't appreciate the gesture for what it was." She handed him the joint.

He tilted his head. "What do you mean?" He took a deep puff.

"I carry more than just a bag of weed in my backpack, you know." She reached inside and dug around for a couple of seconds before pulling out a square zip-up CD case and opening it. She flipped through the CDs it carried like pages in a book until she reached the end, then handed it to him, trading for the joint.

His blood felt like it was boiling as he looked through and recognized all the CDs he had burned for Casey aside from last year's. "Why do you have these?"

"Casey gave them to me." She passed the joint back, grabbed the case from him, zipped it up, and put it back in her backpack.

"I don't understand. Why would she—"

"Because she knew I would appreciate them more. She's not a fan of rock or metal, especially the older stuff. Great taste, by the way." She gave him a thumbs-up.

"You listen to this kind of stuff?" he asked, as though he didn't believe her.

"Of course I do. My dad loved it and played it all the time. This is basically all I ever listen to. It reminds me of him."

"And what? Casey just came and gave them all to you one day?"

"Not exactly. She actually really liked the idea when you did it the first year. She thought it was cute, came to me to ask more about the genres, and we spent hours listening to the songs together. But after the second time, she just wasn't as interested. Listening to it became a chore for her, so she gave them to me once she played through them a few times."

"I . . . I don't believe you," he said.

She smirked and tapped her backpack. "Why else would I have them?"

"Good point." He took a hit from the joint. "But I really don't want to believe you."

"I know, and it sucks, and I'm sorry. I wish I had told you sooner because I really hated seeing how upset you were when she didn't show up. You're too good for her, and you didn't deserve to go through that."

"So you were telling the truth?"

She nodded and reached for the joint. "Yeah, unfortunately. She told me her plan was to break things off this summer before she left for college. I didn't know she was going to do it like this. As soon as I can get ahold of her, I swear I'm gonna yell at her."

"I'm so dumb," he said. Jordan looked at him and frowned before scooting her butt across the dirt and sitting beside him, resting her head on his shoulder.

"No, you're not." She grabbed his hand. "You didn't know."

He felt a lump form in his throat, blocking him from speaking as his eyes watered.

"Am I interrupting?" A man's voice made them both jump as Jordan quickly hid the joint behind her back and Max waved the smoke out of the air. Mitch rolled his wheelchair out from behind a tree.

Max and Jordan looked at each other, both almost certainly thinking the same thing—we are fucked. "No," they said in unison.

He sniffed the air. "It certainly smells like I am. And I know my trusty counselors wouldn't sneak off into the woods to smoke weed and lie to my face about it."

"Of course not," Jordan said.

"Good. You should know I've got a nose for the stuff like a police dog," Mitch said. "So where is it?"

Jordan and Max shot each other an uncomfortable glance. Then she pulled it out from behind her back and held it out like a guilty kid showing a parent the pack of gum they stole from the gas station.

Mitch rolled forward, shaking his head, and grabbed it from her. "Thank you for your honesty."

Max felt like he was at rock bottom. First, he lost his girlfriend, and now his job. His stomach sank until Mitch pulled the joint to his mouth, took a seven-second inhale, and held it in for just as long before blowing it out.

"That's some good shit," he said. "I guess I don't have to scold you."

Max and Jordan looked at each other again, their eyebrows narrowed in confusion.

"Uh, sir?" Jordan asked.

"What, did you think I was just gonna let my counselors sneak off into the woods and smoke without me?"

Chapter 14

While Annie may not have possessed the same curvaceous figure as Pamela Anderson, she undeniably felt a resemblance when she squeezed into the snug, red one-piece swimsuit she had selected from the options provided for the counselors. It brought about a sense of discomfort, but she made a conscious effort to focus on the positive and use it as a confidence booster. After all, compared to Vera's choice of a revealing two-piece, Annie's swimsuit was considerably more modest.

She had spent the better part of the afternoon lounging atop one of two high lifeguard chairs along the lake while Ale—protecting her wound from infection thanks to George's suggestion—occupied the other chair, and George sunbathed on his back on a towel beside them. Chatting with them, Annie determined that they were both hilarious and great company she was excited to spend the summer getting to know better. Even though Ale was technically one of the kids under their care, she was less than a year younger than them and Annie didn't look at her as a kid. George, however, took his adult title and leadership status into account and played up their age gap good-naturedly to decline her persistent flirtatious advances.

"Hey, George," Ale said.

"Hm?" He opened one eye to look up at her sitting in the chair. The sun beamed down on his face.

Alejandra raised her injured leg over him. "The sun is burning my legs, and that can't be good for my wound. I think rubbing on some sunscreen would make it feel a lot better."

"Good idea." He reached for the white squeeze bottle with the orange lid beside him and offered it to her.

"Oh, well . . . I was kind of hoping I could get someone to put it on for me," she said, a wide smile on her face.

"Annie, do you want the honors?" George asked.

"Uh—"

"Don't answer that," Ale interrupted and pulled her hair over the front side of her left shoulder as she turned back to George. "I was really hoping you could do it. Annie's hands are too small and soft to really rub that lotion in."

Annie looked at her hands. They were small but not soft after so much time in the woods. But she already knew that Ale didn't really care about the condition of the hands rubbing her legs. It was about who was rubbing them.

"No can do." George lay back down and closed his eyes.

"What?"

"Nope. Sorry."

"And why not? You're not going to help one of your desperate campers?"

"See, that's how it starts. Here I am, doing my job and helping a camper. Then a picture of me rubbing this little girl's feet shows up at my boss's doorstep in a manila envelope. Six months later, I'll be in a courtroom defending myself."

"Gosh, are you always this dense?" Ale pouted.

"Hey, being a lifeguard is serious work. I can't have any distractions when I'm watching over this beautiful lake."

"Well maybe the distractions are the best part of the job. I mean, have you seen Annie in that swimsuit? Even I can't stop looking at her. It's hard to focus on anything else," Ale complimented. A confidence booster Annie wasn't expecting.

"It's much easier when you're blocking the view."

"Funny," Ale said. "If it's your lifeguard duty that's turning you into this party pooper, how about you join me tonight for a dip under the moonlight? There won't be any distractions, just the two of us."

"Kids go to bed at nine. Besides, you can't risk your wound getting infected, remember?"

"Then maybe you can tuck me in yourself?"

"You're a big girl, I'm sure you can manage."

"But what if I have nightmares?"

"You'll be just like everyone else in the cabin."

Annie tried her best not to laugh at that one. She had a dark sense of humor, but even that one made her uncomfortable, given the setting.

"But we can avoid that if you crawled into bed with me."

"That wouldn't be fair to the other children."

"You know . . . the way you care so much about these kids can be a big turn-on."

"Hopefully an adult woman will have that same opinion someday."

Ale sighed. "Annie, can you please convince George that I'm not a child?"

Annie held up her hands in an I'm-not-touching-that gesture.

George laughed. "Good luck. Try again in a few years."

"Years? I'll be your age in four months."

"And as far as I'm concerned, you might as well still be drinking from sippy cups and wearing diapers until then."

Ale crossed her arms and sank in her chair as Hailey and Billy approached from the lake.

"A diaper doesn't sound like a bad idea for her tiny bladder," Hailey joked.

"And here I thought you'd make a good wingman," Ale said.

"I'm supposed to help you with your injury, not your love life." Hailey looked at the wrap around Ale's ankle and clicked her tongue when she saw a shade of pink seep-ing through. "You're bleeding through the bandage. We should go to Nurse Cherie and get a new one."

"Okay, fine." Ale held her injured leg out straight and hopped out of the chair onto her good leg while Hailey and Billy put her arms around their shoulders. "I'll be seeing you later," she said to George.

"Do we need to throw you in the water to cool you off?" Billy asked, as they started hobbling away.

"You'd think she was high on painkillers," Hailey added.

Ale responded with something inaudible as Annie watched them move farther away.

"You're popular," Annie said.

"It comes with the territory. When you have a body like mine, people want a piece of you. Men, women, children. Doesn't matter," George said, flexing his pectoral muscles.

"Ew, gross."

"Yeah, that sounded a lot better in my head."

Annie laughed.

"See, my charm is rubbing off on you, too," he said.

"You wish."

"Don't pretend it isn't. Eventually, they all cave."

"You sound like a supervillain." Annie snickered

"Keep laughing, you'll see. Spend enough time around me this summer and you'll understand."

Max rested his head on Jordan's shoulder, tired from the high. She was writing something in the journal Max had seen her with the night before. He was curious about its contents, but the way she awkwardly held it at an angle told him she didn't want him to see.

"Is it lunchtime already?"

"I'm not sure. I'd check my phone but . . ." Jordan trailed off, and they both laughed hysterically before coming to a dead silence as Mitch snored across from them. After a brief pause, their laughing continued. "So tell me . . ."

Max looked up at her.

"Of all the counselors at this camp, you're the only one whose story I've never heard. Is there a reason for that?"

"I'm sure you know how hard it is to talk about that sort of thing." He laughed. "Well maybe you don't. You were so open about it last night."

"No, I get it. But is that it? You just don't like to talk about it? Or have you still not gotten over it?"

"I don't think I'll ever get over it." He sat up straight and spit on the dirt to his left, narrowly missing the two stacked plates from breakfast.

"You know what I mean."

"Yeah. I do. Honestly, I just don't think it needs to be publicly declared around that campfire setting. I only really talk about it with people I'm close to."

She grabbed his arm and pulled herself closer to him, resting her head on his shoulder. "Isn't that why we're out here? I want to get closer to you."

He smiled. Her hands were soft, and her body was warm against his. It felt nice, given the cool breeze he'd put up with for an unknown number of hours. "How about this . . . tell me what you're writing, and I'll tell you my story?"

"Oh, it's nothing really." She closed the journal.

"You sure write a lot in there for it to be nothing."

"Fine, I'll tell you if you promise not to laugh."

"If I laugh, it's the weed," he said, already chuckling.

"Fair enough." She opened the journal to the very first page, which had very little writing and was formatted like a screenplay. "It's just a project I'm working on."

The title was *Jordan's Perfect Slasher Movie,* followed by the author tag *by Jordan Thompson.*

"Jordan's Perfect Slasher Movie," he read out loud, grabbing the journal from her hands. He felt her try to pull it from him, but her resistance wavered almost as quickly as it started. "You're writing a movie?"

"It's just in the outline stage."

"This is awesome," he said, scanning through the pages of notes, scenes, and character bios before ending on a page dedicated to a character named Max.

"Oh! That's—" She tried to reach for the journal, but he pulled it away from her.

"You named a character after me?" he asked, his interest at its peak.

"You have a common name," she said, but her cheeks were flushed red.

"Scrawny but cute and likeable," he read.

"You really don't have to read it." She failed to snatch it from him once again.

"Eventually falls for main character, Jordan"—he looked at her, eyebrows raised, before continuing to read—"but dies before he can confess." He felt offended. "So I'm in love with you, *and* I die?"

She laughed and shrugged her shoulders. "It's a slasher movie."

"But…you wrote me to fall in love with you?" he asked.

She finally snatched the journal from him. "It's not finished yet. Besides, I never said it was about us. That was your assumption."

"You used our names!""

"Placeholders."

"Jordan." He looked into her eyes. "Do you have feelings for me? You can tell me—"

She interrupted him, pushing her finger to his lips. "I showed you what was in my journal, and now it's your turn to hold up your end of the deal."

"But—"

"No *buts*," she interrupted again.

"Okay, fine. *But* we aren't through with this conversation."

"If you say so." She rolled her eyes before closing them with a smile on her face and lying back on the grass.

He felt like he was beginning to tell a lullaby, which was ironic because it was the furthest thing from it. Though, for a girl as into slasher movies as Jordan was, this might actually be the kind of story to put her to sleep.

"During my freshman year, I was hanging out with some friends, waiting at the bus stop. One of them brought up our town's famous abandoned slaughterhouse that wasn't too far from the school. This was a hot spot for kids around my age because there were rumors that this place was haunted. Naturally, this sparked interest in high schoolers that wanted to do some crazy, adventurous, and daring shit. Thinking back, it doesn't sound that cool. But I was stupid—we all were. So when my friend brought it up, it didn't take long for us all to agree that visiting that slaughterhouse in the middle of the night was a great idea."

"So you guys went there?"

"Yeah. Only, the place wasn't haunted . . . or abandoned. At least, not entirely. It had one inhabitant. A homeless man named Rick. People only thought the place was haunted because of the occasional sightings of this man and the disturbing noises he would make while he was fucked-up on drugs. My group of friends was just the first group of people to encounter Rick up close, and he was completely out of his mind. He was a former employee of the slaughterhouse—the only place that would give him work with his drug abuse history since the owner of the place was a close friend of his sponsor. When it closed down, Rick had no other options. He lost his house and had no money, so he took what few things he had and moved into the slaughterhouse. It didn't take long for him to fall off the wagon and let the drugs consume him again.

"He started out taking loans from his dealers to get his fixes, and when they stopped giving him money and he couldn't pay them back, he would find them, rob them of whatever drugs were in their house, kill them, and hide the bodies in the basement of that slaughterhouse. When we arrived that night, he was high out of his mind. He was having a hallucination that he was still working there, and my friends and I were little pigs running around the place. We all got split up when he chased us around with a cleaver. We spent hours trapped, searching for one another while trying to stay hidden."

"Yeah, I can see why you wouldn't want to talk about that," Jordan said, without losing her smile or opening her eyes.

"It was the worst night of my life. I watched two of my friends get slaughtered with my own eyes and found the others in unimaginable states: hanging from meat hooks, hands and feet chopped off like they were hooves, disemboweled. I—" Max started laughing. "God, I can't believe I woke up so mad at you this morning. Now look at us."

"We'll be okay. I shouldn't have been so mean last night. I just couldn't stand seeing you hung up on a girl who couldn't be bothered to let you know she wasn't coming."

"I needed something like that to shake me out of it. A big part of why I was so worried is because I have fucking abandonment issues. If I don't see somebody for a long time, I always worry that I'm going to find them dead."

"I don't blame you." Jordan put her hand on his chest and looked up at him. "You've been through some scary shit."

Without thinking, Max leaned in and kissed her, and she kissed him back. Passionately. He pulled away. "I'm sorry."

She sat up. "Don't be." She grabbed his face and pulled him in for more. Her tongue felt warm as it entered his mouth, grazing the inside of his upper lip. They kept at it until Mitch snored once again and they turned his way, just as he woke up.

"Shit, what time is it?" he asked.

Max and Jordan exchanged looks as they wiped each other's saliva from their mouths onto their wrists.

"Not sure," Jordan said. "We should probably get back."

"The sun is already setting!" Mitch said, looking up at the sky through the trees, then down to his watch. "It's six thirty." He shook his head.

Max looked up and confirmed. The previously blue sky now had an orange tint. "Shit. We were in charge of lunch."

The three of them burst into laughter.

"I'll meet you there," Jordan chuckled. "I'm gonna drop off my bag at the cabin."

Chapter 15

"Welcome back, campers," Mitch said, sitting in front of the campfire. His eyes were tired and bloodshot and he had a noticeable lack of energy from the days before—all traits shared with the counselors from the bear cabin. Traits that Hailey recognized immediately as side effects of weed. "I don't want to take too long with introductions today. So, how is everybody?" He looked around as the crowd applauded and spoke to each other.

Ale murmured, "I've been better," beneath the crowd noise.

Mitch looked confused as he tried to focus on each individual person who responded to his question. "Wow, alrighty then. Sounds like everybody's good. Does anyone have anything they want to share with the camp?

Vera stood up, drawing the attention of everyone in the crowd, including a look at her backside from George, who sat close behind her. Hailey spotted this and glanced at Ale to confirm that they both saw the same thing.

"Can you blame him? I wish I had her ass," Ale said.

"Then maybe you wouldn't have had to try so hard at the lake." Hailey laughed.

"I'll do it, but only because I know you guys are gonna expect a story from me and I just want to get it out of the way," Vera said.

"Awesome, the floor is yours."

"Do you think they're fucking?" Ale asked.

"What?" Billy leaned forward to be within whisper distance. "Who?"

"Vera and George," Hailey whispered, filling him in. She looked at Vera, who looked nervous for the first time since Hailey had met her.

Vera took a glance back at George, who nodded to her as if saying, "It's okay," which was enough to give her the confidence to tell her story. She smiled at him and faced the firepit.

"Shit. They're definitely fucking," Ale lamented.

"So much for that dream," Billy teased, leaning back to his normal seated position.

Ale scoffed. "That won't stop me from trying." She crossed her arms and leaned back.

"I don't doubt that," Hailey said.

Vera continued looking into the fire silently, as if it contained the story she was looking to tell. She sniffled once and cleared her throat. "It happened at the end of eighth grade, the night before my middle school graduation. I threw a slumber party and invited a few girls—my best friends. We heard all these stories about people going to high school and changing. You know, making new friends, moving away, stuff like that. We were worried that it was going to happen to us, so we had a sleepover to celebrate our friendship for what it was, and all that it had been over the years we grew up with each other. It was an in-case-anything-happens going-away party."

She took her seat and George gave her a comforting rub on her shoulder.

"Well, long story short, some lunatic broke into the house that night and attacked us. I won't paint as grue-some a picture as Jordan, but I'm the only one of my friends who survived that night." She brushed her hair out of her face and wiped her eyes. "That's my story." The crowd clapped for her while she continued wiping her face and forcing a smile. Nick, sitting beside her, rubbed her thigh for comfort and George leaned forward to hug her.

"So George has competition?" Ale asked.

"Maybe that's her secret. George probably thought you were too easy," Hailey joked.

"I'm not easy, just . . . desperate?" Ale sounded unsure of herself after the words left her mouth.

Billy stood up.

"Not that desperate," Ale said as the crowd simmered down and focused on him.

"If you don't mind, I'd like to share with the crowd," he said, looking to Mitch for confirmation, but he was dead asleep.

"Of course, please. We would love to hear someone other than the counselors for once," Nick said, stepping up nicely as the head counselor should.

"Seriously?" Ale asked.

"Look at you, all brave and stuff," Hailey joked and gripped his hand.

He shook it, smiled at her, and said, "I want to hear yours next." She smiled back and shook her head." Then, with all eyes on him, he stepped forward to make sure everyone could see him. "Hello, everyone. My name's Billy." He waved.

The crowd quietly replied, "Hi, Billy," as if they were in an Alcoholics Anonymous meeting.

"This is just my second year here at camp and, unfortunately, my last. I'm seventeen and have my senior year coming up, so . . . yeah." He scratched beneath his chin. "This is a bit embarrassing to tell, all things considered, so try not to laugh, I guess."

Ale looked at Hailey, suspenseful.

"Nobody will laugh, Billy."

Max giggled from across the firepit and Jordan smacked his arm, shutting him up—confirming Hailey's belief that they were high.

Billy ignored the slight interruption and began his story. "I was pretty young . . . well, relatively. Definitely too young to have seen this, I guess."

Hailey grabbed his hand from behind and held it. It was the first time she had seen him this nervous. He looked back and smiled, holding her hand while he continued. "I was in the third grade, and my parents took me to a carnival. Just outside the entrance, before we even got our tickets, there was a clown. He was surrounded by children as he tied balloon animals for each of them, free of charge. I ran over to him to get one while my parents waited in line for tickets. He tied a balloon dog for me, and I went right back to my parents as they finished up, then we went into the carnival." He sniffled and looked up. "Long story short, that clown wasn't affiliated with the carnival. He took a sledgehammer and went on a rampage, murdering his way through the carnival." He squeezed Hailey's hand. "My dad died trying to stop him, and because of his sacrifice, I am here today to tell you about it." He walked back to his seat while the crowd clapped for him.

"Thank you for that," Nick said, standing from his seat to take the floor. "Seriously, that was so brave to take the initiative and be the first camper this year to talk about what happened to them."

Billy smiled, though he was on the verge of tears.

"Oh, so he's brave when he tells a gruesome story, but I get criticized for it," Jordan said, sparking a laugh from

Max and a sharp glare from Nick. "Sorry, I'm only joking. Just trying to lighten the mood."

"Please, keep trying." Billy laughed.

"I think that's enough for stories tonight. Everyone, feel free to hang out at the fire for a while longer, but not too long. I don't plan on waking you up early tomorrow, but that doesn't mean you can stay up all night. And that goes for your counselors too. I don't want anyone forming bad sleeping habits on my watch," Nick said.

The campers all immediately began talking to each other as soon as Nick sat back down. Annie and George both turned to the members of the squirrel cabin.

"I'm so sorry to hear that you went through that," Annie said.

"Seriously, what the fuck?" Ale asked. "How are you not way more messed up?"

Hailey smacked Ale's knee.

"That was really great of you to share that with us," George said. "I couldn't talk about what happened to me until after my second year at camp."

"Keeping it short made it easier."

"Still, that was awesome." Hailey smiled. "Not what happened, but that you could talk about it and keep your composure. *You're* awesome," Hailey corrected herself.

"Get a room," Ale joked.

"So what do you guys think?" Annie asked. "Should we stay out here for a while longer, or are you all as tired as I am?"

"Tired," Ale said.

"Yep," Billy agreed.

"Exhausted. That early morning about killed me." Hailey yawned.

"Not to mention that it's cold as shit out here." Ale shivered.

The other campers nodded their heads as Annie scanned over them.

"Okay, so let's get you all to the cabin and you can hang out in there for a while, if you'd like, before going to sleep," George said.

Ale extended her wounded ankle toward George. "I think I need to get an ice pack from Nurse Cherie's office and maybe a new bandage." She retracted her leg. "Do you think you could carry me over there?"

George smirked at her attempt, and Billy piped up to save him, "That's okay, me and Hailey can take you. I want to say hi to Woodsby."

Ale rolled her eyes. "Fine."

The members of the squirrel cabin all stepped away from the firepit while helping Ale.

"Don't stay out too late. I'll be waiting at the cabin for you three to get there to make sure you're okay," George said.

"Yes, sir," Ale said as Hailey and Billy carried her away.

They first entered the cafeteria and hobbled toward Nurse Cherie's office. There were a few campers hanging out at tables inside the dining area, presumably getting away from the cold outdoors.

"Gosh, Billy," Ale said. "You're such a cockblocker. And I can't even be mad at you after that damn story you told."

"It's just hard to see you embarrass yourself like that."

"Do you see my leg?" Ale asked as they approached the door. "I'm already embarrassed. Now let me embrace it."

They opened the door, and Nurse Cherie greeted them with a cheerful grin. "My favorite patient!"

Woodsby's ears pricked up, but he didn't move from his bed.

"Aren't I your only patient?" Ale asked, taking a seat on the stool she had grown accustomed to since stepping on the bear trap.

"You'd be surprised how many of the younger kids think they need to see a nurse when they fall and scrape their elbow," she said, removing Ale's bandage like she had done it a million times before. "Besides, Woodsby is quite pop-ular."

"That . . . makes a lot of sense," Ale said, grimacing at the sight of her ankle. It was much redder than before, and the swelling had only gotten worse. "Ew."

"Yeah, that doesn't look too great. Definitely inflamed, but it doesn't look infected, so that's good. You've been staying off of it, right?" She started wiping the wound with rubbing alcohol.

"Yep. I've been using your crutches when I remember to, but I mostly just have these two carry me around. Makes me feel like a princess."

"Okay, just keep it elevated and ice it at night. I'm going to switch you from regular painkillers to some anti-inflammatory ones. Just take them every six hours or so." She began rewrapping the ankle.

"Yes, please."

"Do you have any medicine that can make her less horny?" Billy asked.

Cherie looked up, taking a pause from the wrapping, confused.

"He's just jealous that I've got eyes for George instead of him," Ale said.

"George? The counselor?" Cherie asked.

Ale nodded.

"How old are you?"

"Coming up on eighteen."

"Well then, I don't blame you. That man looks like he was sculpted by the ancient Greeks," Nurse Cherie said.

Hailey and Ale laughed.

"Nobody's denying that, but Ale is way too vocal about it," Billy said.

"Unfortunately, I don't have any medicine for that."

Woodsby rolled onto his back and yawned.

Chapter 16

Following their trip to Nurse Cherie's office, Hailey, Ale, and Billy trekked back to the squirrel cabin where the other campers were already asleep and crawled into bed.

"Thank you both for helping me out," Ale whispered. "I'm not sure if I said that already.

"I'm sure you would be just as helpful if we were injured," Hailey said.

"That sounded sarcastic." Ale smiled.

"Maybe a little." Hailey giggled.

Ale sighed. "You guys are gonna hate me . . ."

Hailey shook her head. "Don't say it."

"Why would we hate you? Sure, you're pretty high maintenance, but it's really not that bad," Billy said.

"No, not that . . . I have to pee."

"Damn it," Hailey cursed.

"You're joking, right?" Billy hoped.

"Not a joke," Ale said. Billy and Hailey stayed quiet, as if hoping the urge would just go away if they didn't acknowledge it. But sure enough, it didn't. "Can you guys help me?"

"Why didn't you go on the way back from the nurse's office?" Billy asked.

"I didn't have to go then."

"Of course you didn't." Hailey threw off her covers and settled Lana atop her pillow. "Let's go."

Billy got to Ale's side just as Hailey reached the bottom of the ladder. They helped her out of bed and walked to the cabin door, where Billy pulled out the flashlight Nurse Cherie had given him and turned it on once they were outside.

They traveled carefully to the bathroom, kicking leaves out of their path and scanning the ground for traps along the way. In the distance, a dog barked.

"Did you guys hear that?" Billy stopped and pointed the flashlight toward the sound.

"Was it a bark?" Hailey asked.

"I think so." Billy brought the flashlight back toward the path in front of them and continued walking.

"It was probably just Woodsby," Ale said, followed by another bark.

"Definitely Woodsby. There aren't any other dogs out here." Hailey reasoned.

Billy shook his head. "That doesn't seem right."

"What? Why not?" Ale asked.

"Woodsby doesn't just bark. He's trained to only bark when someone needs help." Billy stepped up to the bathroom door and held it open for them. "I'll wait out here." Hailey took Ale's weight on her own and helped her through the door.

"He's a dog. Barking is what they do," Ale said.

Hailey walked Ale to the stall and helped her inside. "Are you okay?"

"Yeah, I'll be fine." Ale closed the stall door and Hailey heard it lock. The dog was now barking more aggressively and frequently.

"Hurry in there, will you?" Billy yelled into the bathroom.

"I am!"

"No, take your time. Make sure you get it all out because I am not coming back here tonight," Hailey insisted.

"He's just worried about that dog." The sound of her urinating diminished at the same time the dog stopped barking. "See, the dog's fine!"

"Can we just hurry up and get out of here?" Billy asked. A cold chill rushed through the bathroom as the wind picked up outside.

"Yeah, yeah," Ale said. Hailey heard her rip toilet paper from the roll, then pull her pants up and unlock the door. She rushed to her side and wrapped her arm around her waist when Billy entered the bathroom to help. "Thanks."

"Don't mention it," he said. Ale limped the first few steps until she found her footing and they made it to the door.

Billy reached forward and opened it, screaming, "Shit!" and scaring both girls. Sitting outside, staring at them with his head tilted, was Park Ranger Woodsby.

"It's just Woodsby," Ale said, smacking Billy lightly for scaring her. Woodsby barked at them and stood up.

"Should he be out here like this?" Hailey asked.

"I don't think so," Billy said. Woodsby barked again and ran ten feet from them before turning back and barking their way again.

"Does he want us to follow him?" Hailey asked.

"He does."

"Seriously? He's just lost," Ale said.

"No, he's not. He knows his way around the camp. Nurse Cherie told us last year that support dogs are trained to look for help if something has happened to their owner."

"Do you think something bad happened?" Hailey asked.

"I sure hope not. Either way, we need to follow him." Woodsby barked a few more times, prancing in place like he was growing impatient.

"Uh, hello?" Ale stuck out her injured foot. "Walking isn't really easy for me right now."

"Yeah, but—" Billy started.

"It's okay. I'll follow Woodsby, and you take Ale back to the cabin," Hailey said.

"No, I'll go." Billy offered.

"I don't feel like lifting her anymore today. It's your turn," Hailey said.

"Hey!" she yelled.

"Okay, well, at least take this." Billy gave her the flashlight.

"No, you guys need it. Ale got lucky with the last bear trap; I'd hate to see her get caught in another one," Hailey said.

"We already checked the route on the way here, so we should be fine. Besides, you might need a light to see what Woodsby is trying to show you." Billy reasoned.

Hailey thought about it and decided he had a good point. She grabbed the flashlight and turned it on. "Thank you."

Billy nodded, and Woodsby barked again. "Okay, you should go."

Hailey watched them turn and walk back toward the cabin. Then she approached Woodsby, and he jumped with worried excitement before leading the way. She followed him as he sprinted at full speed through the woods, stopping every thirty yards or so to make sure Hailey could catch up. Along the way, Hailey saw the counselors' shower building in the distance with its light on.

Woodsby guided her directly across the firepit yard to the main building, where they proceeded through the cafeteria and into the nurse's office. As Hailey opened the door, a putrid stench wafted toward her. The office was in complete disarray, with papers scattered across the desk, the chair toppled over, the medicine cabinet wide open and completely empty, and blood splattered across the wooden walls.

"Oh my God," Hailey said. Woodsby nudged her with his nose as if telling her to investigate further, and as she looked down at him, she noticed the pool of blood emerging from beneath the door and traveling toward her feet. Woodsby stepped through the blood to enter the office and struggled to pull what was behind the door. When he couldn't do it, he looked at Hailey and cried, but she felt too petrified to step inside and confirm what she believed Woodsby was trying to show her.

Reluctantly, she stepped over the crimson puddle, grabbed the doorknob, looked at Woodsby for one last boost of confidence, checked behind the door, and screamed a scream she hadn't mustered in many years.

"It better work this time," Annie said, unhooking her bra. "This is my third night here and I still haven't had a proper, peaceful shower."

"Third time's a charm, right?" Jenna grinned, stepping out of her pants.

"Fuck that. I say we rent a hotel room and sneak off in the middle of the night, just to remind ourselves what hot water feels like," Vera said, neatly placing her removed clothing on the counter.

"I'll pitch in!" Jenna exclaimed.

"Let me know how much and I'll pay it," Annie said. It was just the three of them hitting the showers tonight since Jordan never returned with Max after putting the bear cabin to bed.

The girls headed to their individual stalls, and Annie entered one of them. She closed her eyes and took a deep breath as she pulled the shower chain. As the water cascaded over her body, she couldn't help but let out a small squeal that resonated through the bathroom.

"Sounds like your stall works," Jenna called out. Both of the other stalls sounded as though they were working just as well.

"Thank God," Annie said, making sure her body was wet before squirting her body wash into her hand. She lathered her arms and torso before the water stopped and pulled the chain to rinse it off.

"Hey, Vera," Jenna said, breaking the brief silence.

"What?"

"Were you okay with telling everyone your story tonight? I don't mean to pry, but I couldn't shake the feeling that you got a little flustered toward the end."

"It was fine. Glad I got it over with." She sighed as her water stopped, and she pulled her chain.

"Just . . . if you need anything or want to talk more about it, I'm here." Jenna offered.

"Trust me, I'm fine. I'm one of the counselors, remember?"

"Okay," Jenna said.

"So I hate to ask, but I'm curious. You don't have to answer if it makes you uncomfortable," Annie said. Vera stayed silent, waiting for her to ask the question. "Who was it that attacked you guys? I mean, was it just a random person off the street, or did they have a serious motive?"

"Oh . . ." Vera went quiet long enough for Annie's shower water to stop running. She used the time to lather her legs while Vera answered, "He was our soccer team coach. Some really gross creep who had an obsession with the girls on his team. He went to the house that night to spy on us, and when we caught him, he freaked out and got violent."

Annie could hear the pain in her voice. "Oh my gosh, I'm so sorry."

"Don't be. But let's talk about something else."

"Of course—" The door to the bathroom swung open and slammed against the wall, interrupting Annie.

"Hello?" a familiar girl's voice rang through the bathroom. She sounded worried. The counselors peeked out of their stalls and saw Hailey standing in the doorway—sweaty, out of breath, and her hands and clothes covered in blood.

"Hailey?" Annie pulled her towel down and held it to her chest, letting it hang to cover her front side as she ran to her, only to drop that towel to grab her hands and inspect every inch of them. "What happened? Are you hurt?"

"She, she, she," Hailey stammered as Vera and Jenna surrounded them, lifting her arms and inspecting Hailey's clothes for cuts or signs of a wound as the counselors tried their best to avoid slipping on the puddle on the floor from the water dripping off their naked bodies.

"Who?" Vera asked, an expression of worry and fear drawn on her face

"I don't see any cuts," Jenna said.

"Nurse Cherie," Hailey muttered, her face tired and otherwise void of any emotion. She looked like a shell of herself.

"Good idea. We'll have her check you out." Annie bent down to pick up her towel.

"She's dead," Hailey said, freezing the room as if time had stopped.

The counselors stood motionless, their gaze locked on her, almost expecting her to lose her composure and burst into laughter. Time seemed to stretch on indefinitely until the bathroom door creaked open, unleashing a chilling gust of wind even colder than the dreaded shower water Annie despised.

"I heard a scream," Billy said, stopping short in the doorway, gawking at the scene: three naked counselors surrounding his cabinmate—something straight out of a teenage summer camp attendee's wet dream. "Shit, sorry." He turned his head just enough to seem as if he was trying not to look, then gave up the facade when Hailey turned around and he saw the blood. "Oh my God, what happened?"

He dashed into the bathroom and as the counselors did instinctively, inspected her arms and clothing. Meanwhile, Annie hastily covered herself with her towel and followed Jenna and Vera, who rushed to put on their clothes. Knowing the situation, they understood there wouldn't be enough time to dry off.

"Nurse Cherie is dead," Hailey reiterated, a lot more confident this time.

"What?" Billy asked.

"What do you mean 'She's dead'?" Annie asked, pulling her shirt over her bare chest.

"In her office, I found her. She . . ."

"Come on, let's go check it out," Jenna said, pulling on her pants and reaching for her shoes. The counselors finished getting dressed and ran for the exit.

Annie turned to Billy before running out and said, "Stay with her."

He appeared simultaneously confused, worried, and scared, but then he recognized his responsibility. Overcoming his fear, he confidently nodded and pulled Hailey close while Annie made her way through the door. As they hurried through the camp, Annie noticed the evident fear in the other girls, a reminder of emotions they had previously endured but that she was fortunate enough to have avoided.

When they entered the cafeteria, Woodsby exited the nurse's office and growled, only to chuff at them upon seeing who they were and go back inside. The first sign of blood they saw were the red paw prints Woodsby left for them, leading into the room where they came upon the disaster within. Annie ran in first, leaving the other two who were shaking at the knees just outside. She went straight to where Woodsby was pointing his bloodstained nose—behind the door.

"Oh my God," she whispered, dropping to her knees beside Nurse Cherie's body. She reached for her neck to feel for a pulse like she had seen done in so many movies, but once she pulled the sticky and matted hair out of the way, she saw the deep slit across her throat that had caused the mess she was now squatting in.

"Is she—" Jenna tried to step inside, but Annie held out her arms to stop her.

"Don't come in here. It's bad. Hailey was right," Annie said.

"No!" Jenna banged her head against the wall and slid down to sit on her butt. Vera collapsed to the floor holding both her shoulders, then curled up in the fetal position.

Annie just looked at Nurse Cherie, unsure of what she needed to do next. She hadn't seen a dead body before and had only heard about things like this from her fellow counselors, two of whom seemed to be out of commission at the moment. She started by closing Cherie's eyes, because the way they stared blankly at nothing made Annie feel a lot more uncomfortable about the realism of death. Then, after a sudden realization, she jumped to her feet and started gathering the girls and helping them up.

"Come on, we need to get help," she said.

"Yeah, you're right." Jenna stood up, one leg at a time.

"You guys go." Vera rolled to her back, still shaking. "I'm . . . I'm good here."

"No, it's not safe." Annie reached for her arm and both Vera and Jenna looked at her with morbid curiosity.

"What do you mean 'it's not safe'?" Jenna asked. Vera stared at Annie with a look of absolute terror, as if she was scared to death of the answer.

"Cherie, she . . . she's not just dead," Annie said. Jenna tilted her head, already assuming what she had meant. "She was murdered."

"No," Jenna said.

"Not again." Vera sat up and hugged her knees. Tears began to pour from her eyes. "I can't go through this another time."

"I know, I know, but all that matters is getting help right now," Annie said, shaking her extended hand to emphasize that Vera needed to take it. She reached for it and pulled herself up with a flaccid grip.

Annie took one last glance at Woodsby, who sat in the pool of blood in the office, saddened by his owner's passing, before leading the way back to their cabin.

Chapter 17

Annie opened the door to the counselors' cabin and turned on the light. Nick and George were awake, lying in bed, wondering why she turned on the light. Neil was still asleep in his bed. Jordan and Max were nowhere to be found.

"What the hell?" Nick asked.

"At least warn me before you turn that on," George said, blinking his eyes hard to let them focus. Then he noticed the girls were stressed out. "What's going on?"

"Get up and put some clothes on," Annie said.

"That's the first time I've heard that," George joked.

"This isn't the time for fucking games," Vera said, scratching her head like she was trying to wake herself from this nightmare. George looked offended.

"Annie, what's the matter?" Nick asked.

"Someone killed Nurse Cherie."

"What?" George asked.

"God, do you fucking listen?" Vera paced the room. Her chest heaved as she breathed.

"It's true," Jenna said. "One of your campers found her in the nurse's office."

"Her throat was slit. There was blood everywhere. Oh my God." Annie felt a wave of nausea as she envisioned the scene again. She ran out of the cabin and puked into the bush below the light by the door. She wiped her face and stepped back inside. The guys—minus Neil, who was still asleep—had gotten out of bed.

"Neil, wake up." Nick shook him while George put a shirt on.

"Huh? What?"

"Wake up! There's been a murder," Nick said. Alarmed, Neil sat straight up and scanned the faces of everyone in the room, as if he was remembering where he was at the same time. He checked to see if they were joking.

"For real?" he asked.

"Yes!" the girls and Nick yelled while George shook his head.

"What are we gonna do?" Vera asked, taking a seat on her bed. Annie leaned against her bed, resting her head on the frame of the top bunk and closing her eyes, hoping it would help clear the image of the look on Cherie's face from her mind, but it only made her see it more vividly.

"We need to make a plan," George said. "Does anyone else know?"

Annie shook her head. "Just Hailey and Billy from our cabin. Unless they went back to the cabin and told everyone."

"Went back?" Nick asked.

"We left them at the counselors' showers. Hailey was the camper who found the body, and she was in rough shape. I told Billy to stay with her," Annie explained.

"Okay, someone needs to go make sure they're still there," George said.

"We can do that." Annie volunteered.

"You can do that. I'm sitting right here," Vera declared.

"So am I," Neil said as he munched on a bag of chips he pulled from beneath his pillow. "I mean, I'll stay put to keep her safe.

George sighed.

"I'll go with you," Jenna said.

"No, you stay here with Vera and Neil. Strength in numbers. I'll go with Annie. It would be safer to have a guy go with you." George turned to Jenna and said, "No offense."

"None taken. I'm tired of running around the camp tonight."

"Besides, they're our campers anyway." George held his finger to his chin like he was deep in thought about what else needed to be done. "Annie, when we find them, we need to bring them back here or at least tell them not to tell anyone else. We don't want to cause alarm within the camp. A bunch of kids having PTSD episodes would be the worst thing to happen in a situation like this."

"Tell me about it," Vera said, lying on her bed and pulling the blanket over herself.

"I'll go grab the phones. They're in one of the storage closets in the cafeteria." Nick headed for the door.

"That's a good idea," George said. "Do you want to wait for me to get back?"

"No. It's a mostly lit path and I'll run. I'll likely be back before you guys."

"Here." George reached beneath his mattress and pulled out a pocketknife he had hidden there. "Take this and be careful. Don't trust anyone. Get the phones and get back here. If you're not back before us, we will go looking for you."

Nick took the knife and examined it like he wanted to reprimand him for having it. Obviously knives were a big no-no at this camp. "Thank you."

"When you get there, don't look in the office if you have a queasy stomach," Annie said.

"Noted. Good luck."

"You, too," George said as Nick left the cabin. "Are you ready to go, Annie?"

"Yeah. Let's do this."

"If anything happens while we're gone, grab a whistle hanging here by the door and fucking blow as hard as you can." George pointed to the whistles.

"I'll probably just scream," Jenna said.

Vera agreed. "Same. I'm pretty good at that by now."

George concealed his smirk, his mind momentarily wandering to a potential sexual innuendo before he refocused on the seriousness of their present circumstances. He swiftly picked up one of the dangling whistles, placed it around his neck, and confidently took the lead.

"Hello?" Annie called into the seemingly empty shower room. The timer light switch had five minutes remaining, which told her that somebody had recently touched it. "It's me, Annie."

From behind the curtain of the stall farthest from the door, Billy peeked his head out and let out a sigh of relief before retracting his head back into the shower. "Hailey, Annie's back."

Annie and George rushed to the stall and pulled open the curtain. They were both seated on the floor with Billy's arm wrapped around Hailey. She yawned and stretched her arms like she'd just woken up from the best sleep she'd had in a long time.

"I'm glad you guys are okay," George said.

"Did you find her?" Hailey asked.

"Yeah, I did," Annie confirmed. Billy looked disappointed, as if he'd hoped the answer was no, even though Hailey's embrace had stained his shirt red with blood that wasn't from either of them.

"Let's go. We're going to take you two to our cabin so you're safe while we plan out what happens next," George instructed.

"We can't leave Ale. She's at the squirrel cabin, and she's probably worried about us," Billy said.

"That's not an option. We need to keep this secret until the police get here. We can't have all the campers freaking out and running around in the middle of the night," George insisted.

Billy countered. "But she's probably freaking out already. We both heard Hailey screaming, and I had to leave her behind. She could wake up the other campers in the cabin to tell them something weird is going on."

George sighed. "You're right. But don't tell her what's going on until we're away from the other campers. And be quiet. Get in and get out."

They cautiously walked through the woods to the squirrel cabin, where the lights remained off and the campers were silent. George opened the door and stepped inside.

"Billy?" Ale whispered. She noticed it was George and sat up from her bed. "George?" She seemed confused but shuffled her hair, fixing it.

"Ale, quick. Come with us," George said. He picked up her crutches from the floor and held them up for her to use.

"What's going on?" she asked, but George only responded by holding one finger to his lips, shushing her. She obeyed, and he helped her up to the crutches and they left the cabin. Annie closed the door behind them, twisting the knob so it wouldn't make a sound.

"Will one of you tell me what's going on?" Ale asked, crutching over to her cabinmates. She noticed the mess on Hailey's arm and clothes. "Is that fucking blood?"

"Quiet down," Billy urged. "We don't want to make a commotion."

"We'll tell you on the way," George said.

"On the way? Where are we going?"

"To the counselors' cabin," Annie answered, leading the way.

Once they gained some distance from the cabin, George said, "Nurse Cherie was murdered." Hailey looked especially upset, having heard it again.

"I'm sorry, what?" Ale asked loudly.

"*Shh!*" Billy held a finger to his lips.

"Quiet, remember?" Annie asked rhetorically.

Ale looked at Hailey for confirmation. "Are they serious?"

Hailey just held up her hands, emphasizing the blood on them.

Alejandra's face fell, and she was rendered speechless for the first time since she'd arrived at camp.

"We're going back to our cabin so we can devise a plan," Annie explained.

"A plan? Call the fucking police, that's the plan."

"Nick should be calling them now," George said. "But we don't know who the killer is, and the police won't be here for a while. We have to figure out what to do next."

"You don't know who the killer is? What do you mean you don't know?" She looked at each of them frantically. "How do you even know she was murdered?"

"Her throat was slit," Annie said, sparing the gory details as the horrific image of the scene replayed in her mind. They approached the cabin.

"And you . . ."—Ale looked at Hailey—"you found her?" Her jaw quivered as she realized what Hailey must be going through, witnessing something like that. "Oh my God."

"Let's just get inside and figure out the rest." George opened the door.

Inside, Neil was asleep and snoring and Jenna lay in bed consoling Vera, who was so still she looked like she was sleeping with her eyes open. But Annie knew that although she was awake, she was still experiencing a nightmare. They all were.

"You're back!" Jenna exclaimed, rising from the bed. She saw the campers entering the cabin behind them. "Thank God."

"Where's Nick?" George asked.

"He hasn't gotten back yet. "No Max or Jordan either."

"God damn it. "I'm gonna go look—" Just as George prepared to exit the cabin, Nick walked up to the door. He was empty-handed and looked frustrated. "Where are the phones?"

"They weren't there," Nick replied, shaking his head.

"What do you mean 'They weren't there'?" Annie asked.

"The closet was completely empty. Every phone belonging to the counselors and the campers is gone," he said.

"So nobody's called the police yet?" Ale asked.

Nick shook his head.

"Wait, isn't there a landline in the cafeteria? I've seen Mitch and Betty use it before," Jenna said.

Nick continued shaking his head. "Trust me, I tried. The line's been cut."

"Of course it has." Vera laughed, sitting up from her bed. "Straight out of a slasher movie. Jordan would have the time of her life if she were here right now."

"Yeah, speaking of . . . Where is she?" Nick asked.

"It doesn't matter. We need to get help, and I'm not gonna sit around and wait for more people to die." George started for the door.

"Where are you going?" Nick asked.

"I'm getting in my car and driving for help."

"Do you want me to come with you?"

"I'll be fine. I dare someone to come at me with a knife. They won't like what happens to 'em." With that, he left the cabin, running toward the parking lot.

"How is he even more attractive during a life-or-death situation?" Ale asked.

"Because your body's natural response to most things is aggressive horniness, apparently," Billy answered.

"Gross," Annie said.

"Why don't you guys make yourselves comfortable? Please, take a seat on a bed or something. You must be so tired," Nick said to the campers.

"Great idea," Ale said, following Billy and Hailey to Annie's bed and sitting on the bottom bunk beside each other. Annie took a seat behind them while Nick paced around the room.

"Only three people knew where the phones were," Vera informed the room.

"Huh?" Nick asked, looking at her.

"You, Mitch, and Jordan," Vera said. Nick looked confused. "Don't be so shocked. Jordan told us she had the key. But it was only you three that knew where they were, right?"

"Yeah, that's right."

"Then it's safe to say you three would be the suspects." Vera rationalized.

"Hey, let's not point fingers," Annie said. "We don't know what's going on. The police will get here and figure it out. We aren't detectives."

"But I am right, and you bet that's the first bit of information I'm going to the cops with."

"I don't blame you, Vera. But for now, we need to find out where Jordan and Max are and make sure they're safe," Nick said.

"I doubt they are. Well, Max, anyway. Jordan's right at the top of my suspect list. She is way too into those slasher movies and probably wanted to make one of her own." Vera surmised.

"I seriously doubt that," Jenna said.

"We'll see. For now, we wait."

"That was fast," Annie said to George as he returned to the cabin with a frustrated look on his face.

"What's wrong?" Jenna asked.

George relayed the bad news. "Leaving in a car is no longer an option."

Nick stood from the bed and yelled, "What?"

"They slashed all the tires."

"All of them?" Vera asked.

"Yes. Every tire on every car in that parking lot is done for."

"You've gotta be joking," Billy said incredulously.

"I wish I was."

"Whoever's doing it . . . it sounds like they didn't plan on stopping with Nurse Cherie," Jenna said.

"First the phones, and now the cars. They want us all stuck here," Annie said.

"That much is obvious, but we need to figure out what we're going to do," Nick said.

"We don't have another choice. We're gonna have to round up all the campers. It's not safe for them out there," Annie urged.

"And what are we gonna tell them? They're gonna freak out," Billy said.

"Then they'll be just like the rest of us," Hailey intoned.

"We don't have to tell them anything," George said.

"We could lie to them. Tell them there's a bear in the camp or that Mitch is doing some bullshit survival exercise," Vera proposed.

"That's a good idea," Annie agreed.

"We're gonna have to split up," Jenna said. Everyone looked at her like she was stupid.

"Haven't you heard anything from Jordan, like, ever?" Vera asked. "She always jokes about us being in a slasher movie, but this is the real deal. Splitting up is a terrible idea."

"George sided with Jenna. "We don't know where the killer is. It would be safest and fastest to gather all the campers if we split up."

"Safest for the campers, maybe, but not safest for me when I get stuck in the woods with the killer. Sure, we don't know where the killer is, but we also don't know who they are. It's probably somebody in this cabin," Vera suggested.

George shrugged his shoulders. "We don't have any other options."

Vera looked around the room at the other counselors, who were all in agreement. "Okay, fine. But if I'm going with anyone, I'm going with Neil. At least I can outrun him."

Neil responded with a loud snore as he rolled over, nearly falling off the bed that was too small for him.

"You're not going with anyone," Nick said.

"Excuse me?"

"Someone needs to escort these three campers to our meet-up spot." Nick pointed at Hailey, Billy, and Ale. "I think Annie should do it since George can handle himself by gathering the squirrel cabin's campers." George gave him a thumbs-up and Annie nodded. "Since Jordan and

Max are still MIA, Jenna should gather the campers from the bear cabin and leave Neil with the simple task of the kids in the fish cabin. Vera, you'll be in charge of the eagle cabin."

"Yeah? And what are you going to do?" she asked.

"I'm going to look for Mitch, Betty, and the other counselors," he said.

"Sounds like a plan to me." George nodded his approval.

Jenna was apprehensive. "It sounds dangerous."

"It sounds stupid," Vera snarked.

"So where will we all meet?" Annie wanted to know.

"The cafeteria," George answered. "It's the center of camp and it can fit all of us. Plus, it has lights and walls. People will feel safe there."

"And what do we tell the campers?" Vera asked.

"Whatever gets them to follow you. Now come on, let's go," George said.

Chapter 18

"How long do you think they're going to be?" Ale asked.

Annie wasn't sure. She prayed everything would go smoothly—the counselors and campers would all show up and wait out the night in the cafeteria until they figured out how to get a hold of emergency services. But she knew it was a stretch. Right now, she needed to focus on making life as easy as possible for the campers and making sure they survived the night. "Hopefully not long.

"Some cabins are pretty far from here. Plus, I imagine the campers not wanting to wake up and go for a walk at this hour," Billy said.

"I just hope they all make it safely." Hailey crossed her fingers.

Annie noticed that her eyes kept glancing toward the area where blood had pooled in the cafeteria. She grabbed a tablecloth from a table, closed the door to the nurse's office, and laid the tablecloth over the blood to hide it before the campers arrived.

"Great idea," Ale said. "Looking over there made me feel sick to my stomach."

Annie walked back to them and took a seat on the floor, forming a circle with the four of them as they sat in the back left corner of the room, to the left of the kitchen door.

Ale clutched her ankle and winced.

"Are you okay?" Billy asked.

"Yeah, it just burns."

"That doesn't sound good," Hailey said.

Annie leaned in and pulled up Ale's pajama pant leg to get a better look at it. The wrap had gotten dirty, and the wound had bled through it. "It doesn't look good either."

"Yikes," Billy said. "It's probably infected."

Ale looked toward the nurse's office. "Should . . . should we change the bandage?"

Annie followed her gaze to the office. It was the last place she wanted to go, but her camper was in need and in pain. "Yeah, I'll go grab you a new one." Annie stood up.

"Are you sure?" Hailey asked, almost reaching to stop her.

"I'll be quick." She approached the door and Woodsby followed. Attempting to be cautious with opening it, she encountered slight resistance, fully aware that Cherie's body was right behind it. She put some weight against the door and it opened more forcefully than she intended. When it swung open, she felt it hit Cherie's hand on the other side. Woodsby let out a *woof*.

Annie bit her tongue and winced. She was careful to step over the blood, then moved with haste when she entered the room so she could grab everything necessary before campers arrived and freaked out at the mess inside the office. She found a roll of bandage wrap on the floor beside a knocked over chair and grabbed a bottle of rubbing alcohol, a bag of cotton balls, and a hand towel from the medicine cabinet.

Before leaving, she looked around the room one last time to see if there was anything else they might find useful. She settled on a pair of sharp scissors on the desk, partially to help with cutting the bandage and partially so she would have something to defend herself with if the unknown assailant tried to attack them.

When she got back to Ale, Billy was helping her unwrap the bandage. Ale was squeezing Hailey's hand to help numb the pain, but it was more of a precaution because she was handling it quite well.

"How's it look?" Annie asked as Billy finished pulling it off. Woodsby growled as if the sight of her injury upset him. Dried and dirtied blood covered her wound, the surrounding flesh bright red and swollen.

"Ew!" Ale yelled, looking away.

"Shouldn't it be healing by now?" Billy asked.

"Not necessarily. She's been moving around too much since the incident," Annie said. "Here, let me—" She moved closer, holding the rubbing alcohol and towel, implying that she needed to clean it.

"Right," Billy said, moving away.

Annie opened the rubbing alcohol and held a cotton ball to its mouth, tilting the bottle to soak it. "Okay, Ale, I need you to hold still. This might sting a bit."

"Of course it will," she said, gripping Hailey's hand tighter. Hailey gritted her teeth, like the squeezing was hurting her, but she held her tongue.

She's a good friend, Annie thought as she brought the cotton ball to Ale's ankle and pressed it against the dried mess, cleaning it with surprising ease, although Ale didn't enjoy it very much. She sucked air through her teeth and yanked Hailey's hand close to her chest as she tightened her grip.

"Fucking hell!"

"I know, I know. But we have to clean it. You've been walking around the woods all night and this is about five minutes away from a maggot infestation," Annie said, tossing the dirty cotton ball aside and prepping another.

"What?" She gripped tighter, and Hailey laughed. "She's joking, right?"

"Sure . . ."

Annie repeated the process with a new cotton ball and cleaned up most of the debris surrounding the wound, revealing a cut that looked as fresh as it did the day before.

"So, what do you think?" Billy asked.

"Huh?" Annie continued drying off her ankle with the hand towel.

"That bear trap . . . Do you think Nurse Cherie's murderer was the one who set it up?"

Alejandra sat up, alert. "What?"

"It's possible." Hailey shrugged.

"You mean I could've been a target?" Ale asked.

"I wouldn't say a *target*, but a victim, yes," Billy said.

"It doesn't matter," Annie said as she started wrapping Ale's freshly cleaned ankle. "Whoever did it. . . They'll get caught and pay for it. What matters now is surviving and making sure everyone else does the same."

"Yeah, but—" Ale started.

"She's right," Hailey interrupted. "Let's just focus on right now and pay attention to our surroundings. Obviously we can't trust anyone at camp, but I'd like to think none of us could've done something like that." Hailey pointed to the nurse's office. "We need to stick together and monitor everyone who comes through that door." She moved her pointing finger to the cafeteria's entrance just as George opened it and herded the remaining squirrel campers inside.

"Come on, kids. This is where Mitch wants us to hide for the drill," George said, but Annie understood he was only declaring it loudly enough for her and the other campers to catch on to the lie he told them. But they all looked too tired to ask questions anyway.

"Can we trust him, at least?" Ale whispered to Hailey.

"I hope so. "Just don't let yourself be too vulnerable and do not be alone with anyone."

"Watch me," Ale said, as George and the campers joined them in their small circle that was now a full crowd. A couple of campers even lay flat on the floor and closed their eyes.

"How's it going over here?" George asked.

"Just . . . patiently waiting for this to all be over," Annie said, cherry-picking her words to not alert any campers.

George brought his gaze to Nurse Cherie's office—his first time being this close to the scene since it happened—and glanced away. "Yeah, me too."

The cafeteria door opened again. This time, it was Vera bringing in the campers from the eagle cabin. George ran to assist her with guiding them inside as she was rushing the kids with her face filled with impatience and fear. "Come on, we don't have all night!" The campers looked just as annoyed with her as they were confused.

"Are you gonna tell us what's going on?" asked one of them.

George looked at Vera. "You didn't tell them?" Vera shook her head as if she didn't think she had to. George sighed, then Jenna entered the cafeteria with the bear cabin's campers. "Hello, campers. Take a seat at one of the tables, please," George spoke loudly, as though he was the headman in charge. "Did you guys make sure all the campers are here?"

Vera rolled her eyes. "Of course."

"I'm not sure how many are supposed to be in the bear cabin to begin with, but I asked the campers and they all said nobody was missing," Jenna replied.

"Okay, good."

The campers took their places around the cafeteria tables, filling up almost all the seats as Neil arrived with the final group, the fish cabin. Then they let the campers decide between mingling and sleeping while those who were aware of what was really going on all hung out in the room's corner by the kitchen door. Woodsby made the tablecloth by the nurse's office his bed for the evening, and the counselors told everyone to stay away from him and the office because he was medicated and might attack them if they got too close. None of them questioned this story.

"God, where the hell are the other counselors? At least Nick should be back by now." George was clearly growing more frustrated by the second.

"Nick probably hasn't found them yet. I wonder if Betty and Mitch left the camp," Jenna said.

"Before or after their tires were slashed?" Vera asked. "With our luck, Jordan finished killing Max and Nick was her next victim."

"Quiet down," George warned, looking back at the room full of campers. None of them seemed to have heard her. "You're talking way too loud right now. Jordan didn't"—he leaned in and whispered—"kill anyone. Okay?"

Vera raised her eyebrows in a rebellious "Whatever" and turned away.

"Okay, you know what?" George stood from their circle. "Fuck this. I'm gonna look around and figure something out."

"Like what?" Vera asked.

"I'm not sure, but I'll find something. I'm not gonna sit back and wait for *that*"—he pointed in the direction of the nurse's office—"to happen again." Then he stormed toward the door.

"George, wait!" Annie yelled, louder than she intended. When some of the unaware campers looked at them, she had to rethink what she was going to say because "It's not safe out there" wasn't something one said when trying not to freak out a bunch of traumatized kids.

Before she thought of what to say, George issued an order. "You guys stay here. Nobody else leaves the cafeteria." Then he left.

Chapter 19

Did we really just do that? Jordan thought.

"Remember when I asked you earlier"—Max lifted his butt to slide on his boxers—"if you had feelings for me?"

Jordan looked at him, her head resting on her hand as she lay naked beside him.

"I think I got my answer," he said, a confident smirk on his face.

"Do one-night stands always require feelings?" she asked.

He laughed. "One night? You don't think this will happen again?"

She looked his body up and down. "What do *you* think?" she asked, keeping her tone playful enough for him to catch that she was only teasing. Living the past few years of her life with her guard up to most people, projecting this tough exterior, she found it hard to openly admit she enjoyed herself. Even in a moment as monumental as this—*both* of them losing their virginity—she struggled to show her emotionally vulnerable side to him. Showing her physically vulnerable side, however, was another story. She had never shown her body to a boy like this before, and the way he looked at her filled her with excitement she didn't know was possible.

"I think you enjoyed yourself, and you won't be able to act like you didn't for the whole summer," he said.

He was right. She did enjoy herself—almost too much. So much so that she wasn't even thinking about the rest of the summer; she was thinking about getting through the night without asking to go again.

Physically, the act was quick and . . . okay. She assumed that part was probably better for him, as he just seemed so excited to be there. But the fact that they even did it excited her way more than the actual doing. Vera once warned her that her first time would be painful and not enjoyable at all; she was just partially right. Pain was there, sure, but she had been through worse. She hated using the metaphor, but this *stabbing* was nothing compared to the actual one she had survived.

Regardless, Max made it as enjoyable for her as he could. As soon as her clothes were off, he couldn't stop staring. And not just in one specific place, he looked at her everywhere—places nobody had ever seen before. From head to toe, inch by inch, his eyes traveled around with such intrigue she felt like a work of art that he had been paid to study.

She had a nice figure and she knew it. The amount of both men and women she caught admiring her was uncountable, and that was when she had her clothes on. A healthy diet, morning walks, and the occasional squat or two helped shape that figure, but—as most people do—she still had some insecurities about what hid beneath her clothing, and she feared those would all be confirmed once he ripped her clothes off.

Are my nipples too big for my tits? Would my scars turn a man off? Is my ass firm enough? What does my vagina even look like?

Yet as soon as she saw how he looked at her body—admired it, even—these worries disappeared, and she knew there wouldn't be a problem. Wherever his eyes weren't actively focused, his hands were. That feeling of excitement gave her goose bumps, and he rubbed his hands across those, too, gliding them across her arms, her hips, her ass, her stomach, her breasts, and even her scars. She felt weak in the knees, which made her glad when he invited her to the floor.

"I guess there are worse things I could spend my time doing this summer. Maybe I'll just act like this until you find somewhere more comfortable," she said, looking around at the cramped storage shed they were in. She said it as a joke, knowing full well why this was their place of choice. It was right by the lake, which meant no campers were supposed to be *anywhere* nearby, and there were multiple storage sheds around the camp, so if a counselor needed something it would be highly unlikely they would come to this one.

"Yeah, I was thinking we'd do it in the firepit next time. That would be hot."

She burst out laughing. "You're such a dork," she said, pushing his shoulder.

He kept his eyes on her mouth and smiled as if he was happy seeing her smile, and that made her feel even better. Even though she was completely exposed in front of him, his eyes always knew the right places to be to send jitters through her stomach. He didn't just stare at her like a boy usually would when seeing a naked woman for the first time. It was more like he was seeing through her, directly into her soul, and thoroughly enjoyed what he saw.

"What are you looking at?" she asked nervously.

"You." He leaned in, kissed her on the forehead, and started gathering their clothes scattered around them from the floor.

She grabbed his arm. "What's the rush?"

"The longer we're out here, the more likely someone will come looking for us," he said.

"So let them look. We can relax for a while."

"Aren't you cold?" he asked.

She was. Being right beside the lake, this was the coldest part of camp, and it being the middle of the night didn't help either. "Come warm me up." She tapped the floor beside her.

He smiled and looked to be considering it, then shook his head. "Honestly, I just really have to pee. And you should too. I heard you can get an infection if you don't pee after—"

"Okay, okay, fine," she interrupted. "But for the record, you just gave up a rather obvious sex invitation."

He sighed. "I only brought so many condoms to camp. I'm not sure I want to use them all in one night."

"You know Nurse Cherie hands them out in her office for free, right?"

"I'm sure she does, but not *this* kind." He held up the ripped wrapper from the floor.

She recognized the pattern on the square wrapping from the birth control aisle in the pharmacy: *ribbed for her pleasure*. Of course those would be the kind he bought. Because he was the type to know that he'd be lucky if a girl liked him enough to spread her legs for him, and he would want to treat her right in return. Only the thought of this made her sad because she knew that pleasing her wasn't what he had in mind when he made that purchase. He was thinking of Casey, her best friend. This reminded her of the last conversation she had with Casey prior to returning to Camp Safe Woods.

"I'm gonna do it," Casey said, breaking the long silence on the phone. They had been talking for hours now, sitting in their bedrooms across the state from each other.

"Do what, now?" Jordan asked, focusing on painting her toenails. Black, as she almost always did, or the occasional purple, and even red for when she felt extra adventurous—like she was right now, at camp.

"This summer, I'm gonna sleep with Max."

Jordan paused her paint job and blinked hard at her phone screen, double-checking that it was still Casey she was talking to. "Didn't you say you were finally gonna break that off?"

"Well, yeah. But why not go out with a bang? Literally."

"Wow, that's quite the thought process," Jordan said, stopping herself from declaring her friend crazy. But Casey knew exactly what she was thinking—a testament to their friendship.

"You think I'm crazy, don't you?"

"I didn't say that."

"But you thought it! I could hear it in your voice."

"If only you could hear yourself as well as you hear my thoughts."

"What's that supposed to mean?"

"Breakup sex? Really? I just want you to be careful. Like, what if you get pregnant? I've only ever heard of the guy ditching once the pregnancy's announced, but you'd be leaving him before you even knew."

"I'm not gonna get pregnant! Max is smarter than that. He'll wear a condom."

"Hopefully. I wouldn't tell him you're breaking up until after the deed is done, though. He might try to trap you."

"No, he wouldn't! Max isn't like other guys."

"He sounds like a real keeper, then."

"He is, and I would keep him, but you know how difficult a long-distance relationship would be."

"Yeah, maybe."

"You don't think so?"

"I think relationships take work, and if he's different, like you say he is, then it would be worth it."

Clearly it wasn't, though, because she never came. Seeing how Max's heart broke last night really didn't sit right with Jordan. Sure, he would probably feel worse if she showed up just to leave him, but at the very least, he deserved closure and Casey didn't even grant him that.

Max deserved better, so Jordan gave it to him. At first, she felt bad—almost as if she was betraying Casey—but she didn't want to be with him anyway, and they were barely a relationship to begin with. And now look at him, happier than ever and not a single thought of Casey crossing his mind.

"You know guys can get clingy once they sleep with you," Jordan had told her.

"Bullshit. I only ever hear about guys that hit it and quit it. Like, they'd already called an Uber before they'd even unwrapped the condom," Casey said.

"Yeah, that would be most guys. But you said he's different. This guy, he actually cares about you. Once you give him that next level of connection and trust, I don't know how you're gonna lose him."

Oh God, Jordan thought, *what have I done?*

"Hey, Max," Jordan said.

He looked at her while he pulled up his pants.

"Was this what you really wanted?" Jordan asked.

"What do you mean?"

"We didn't really talk about it."

He looked at her, confused.

"About . . . Casey."

"What about her?"

"Well, tonight," she said. "Was this just some sort of revenge thing? I mean, I get it. If someone hurt me like she hurt you, I'd probably consider fucking their best friend to get back at them. And if that's what this was, I won't be mad, so long as you tell me about it *now*."

"No—"

"And if this is something you plan on doing as a summer only thing like you had with Casey, I just want you to know that I am *not* interested. Don't get me wrong, this was great, and I'd love to do it all summer, but I . . . Well, I'm not sure what I want. But I know I don't want to be *just* a revenge fuck, and I certainly don't want to be a summer fling."

"So you—"

"Yes."

"You didn't even let me finish," he said.

"Because I knew what you were going to ask."

"And that was . . .?"

She rolled her eyes. "You were going to ask me *again*, 'Do you have feelings for me?'"

"And your answer—"

"Yes!" she said, her anxiety reaching an all-time high. She found confessing her genuine feelings somehow harder to do than initiating sex.

He smiled. "Good. Me too."

He leaned in and kissed her. This time felt more magical than their first in the woods just hours earlier. It felt right.

When he pulled away, she just watched as he put the rest of his clothes on and didn't bother with hers until he'd finished. Then she said, "You go first. I'll hang out here for a bit . . . maybe watch the lake for a while. If we both show up at the cabin together at this hour, people might suspect something."

"Good idea." He opened the door and almost stepped out, but he ran back inside to give her one last kiss on the forehead that filled her body with enough warmth to weather the cold air that infiltrated the shed. Then he left.

Chapter 20

After half an hour had passed, almost all the unaware campers had fallen asleep, and Annie was growing restless. George hadn't returned yet. Nick never came back with Mitch or Betty. There was still no sign of Jordan or Max either.

"Are there any blankets in this place?" Ale asked.

"I doubt it, but feel free to go grab some from our cabin," Billy joked.

She flipped him off.

"This'll all be over soon," Annie said. She wanted to cheer them up, but she felt just as helpless as everyone else.

"In one way or another," Vera murmured. Annie didn't care to respond. None of them did. Her negativity was making this experience worse than it already was. Then the door opened.

"Check this out." George stomped into the cafeteria, carrying a familiar composition notebook in his hands. He walked past them and opened the kitchen door, then looked at them like they should've known to follow him.

They all got up and followed him into the kitchen except Neil, who said, "I'll watch the campers."

The room was a lot colder than Annie remembered from when she was helping prep food with Jenna. It may have just been two days ago, but it felt like an eternity.

George paced inside with the book in hand. Annie recognized it as the journal Jordan had been writing in every night before bed.

"Is that . . . Jordan's diary?" Jenna asked.

"Yes!" George yelled. He stopped pacing, opened the book, and started flipping through the pages. "You guys need to hear the stuff she's been writing in this thing."

"I'm not sure I want to. That's an invasion of her privacy," Annie said.

"Where'd you find it?" Vera asked.

"Her bag in the cabin. Does it matter?" George snarled, settling on the page he wanted to show.

"Yes, it does. Were you going through our stuff?" Vera asked.

"Of course I did! Do you think I care about privacy right now? Don't worry, I didn't go sniffing your panties or trying on any of the condoms you brought to camp with you. I went looking for evidence, and I think I found our killer."

"But—"

"Listen to this. This entire book breaks down the steps to a fucking slasher movie, and it sounds awfully familiar to what's going on right now," George said.

"Okay, and—" Jenna tried to chime in and reach for the book, but George pulled away and interrupted.

"Step one: Eliminate any possibility of communication with the outside world. A slasher movie would be cut quite short if the victims could just call the police. Step two: Come up with a reason why they can't just leave the scene. What would the killer do if their target just started their car and drove away?" George read from the book.

"Sounds to me like she was just taking notes or writing an essay. Who fucking cares?" Vera asked.

"I care. This is exactly what the fuck we're going through. She had this whole thing planned out from the start!" George went back to reading, "Step three: Seclusion is key. Come up with multiple possibilities for victims to be vulnerable. Bonus points if they're naked! Showers and skinny-dipping really get a slasher going. Step four: Make sure the counselors all split up. It's a lot easier to pick them off one by one, rather than as a group."

"I'm still not seeing the problem here. She watches a lot of movies. We know this, and she's not wrong! This is just how she vents when nobody else will listen. You know how important therapy is to people like us. That's what this is," Jenna said.

"Step five: Stupid counselors sneak off and have sex while somebody's being murdered." George looked confused as he read the rest of step five. "Max and Jordan sleep together before they realize people are dying?" He finished his sentence like it was a question. Then he looked up from the book as if someone else understood what that sentence meant. But everyone else was just as confused, including Max, who was standing in the doorway, listening.

"Max, where have you been?" George asked.

"What's that?" Max pointed at the book.

"Answer the question, Max."

"Answer mine." He stomped into the cafeteria and ripped the book from George's hands. "Why the hell do you have her diary?"

"Max, calm down," Jenna advised.

"Something happened," Annie added. He looked at her, confused.

"What do you mean? What's going on? And why are all the campers in the cafeteria?"

"Just calm down and listen," Vera said. Everybody quieted. Hailey, Billy, and Ale looked at each other nervously.

"I'm calm. Somebody tell me what's going on," Max insisted.

Annie took a deep breath. She felt like it was her responsibility to fill him in because she was the first counselor to see Nurse Cherie. "Somebody . . . attacked Nurse Cherie."

"What do you mean 'attacked'?"

"She's dead," George answered.

"Her throat was slit open and the corpse is in her office," Vera said.

Max looked around in disbelief, reading the faces of everybody in the room, and he looked emotionless once it struck him that they weren't joking. Then he felt the book in his hand and made the connection. "You guys think Jordan had something to do with it?"

"She's the only one we have evidence on," George rationalized.

"You call this evidence?" Max laughed. "I was with her all night. She didn't kill anybody!" Max said.

"What were you guys doing all night?" George demanded.

Max looked flustered and embarrassed. "It docsn't matter. I was with her," he repeated.

"Was it step five?" Vera pointed to the book and Max pulled it away.

"Fuck you," he said.

"So it was," she gloated.

"Really?" George asked.

"So what? I was with her, so she couldn't have hurt anybody. I mean, seriously. You guys have known Jordan for years. Do you think she would really be capable of something like that?"

"What we think doesn't matter. The stuff she's written in there sounds like she, at the very least, wanted somebody to attack the camp. If she didn't do it herself, she could've assisted," George explained. "Now where is she?"

"I don't know," Max answered, taking a seat on the floor against the wall.

"Bullshit," Vera said, then George raised his hand as if to say, "Let me handle this."

"I know you want to protect her, but you need to tell me where she is." George waited for a response, but Max just looked past him as if he wasn't even there. "Max. If what that book says is true, it sounds to me like she just used you for her little scheme. Whatever went on between the two of you wasn't real. And even if it was, and she isn't responsible for what happened to Nurse Cherie, someone at this camp is, and Jordan is alone out there."

"That's step two, right?" Vera asked, triggering a glare from George insinuating that she wasn't helping.

"It isn't safe for her out there," George said, warranting more silence from Max. When he realized he wasn't gonna get anything from him, he grumbled, "All right," and stormed out of the kitchen.

"We're just gonna let him go?!" Vera exclaimed.

"Are you gonna chase him?" Jenna asked rhetorically.

Vera rolled her eyes and followed George out of the kitchen. Then Jenna and Annie brought their attention to Max, who was now reading through Jordan's diary.

"This is just a project of hers," he said. "A movie she was writing for fun. She showed it to me earlier today. Look." He handed it to Annie.

"So it isn't some evil scheme?" Annie asked, flipping through the pages filled with nothing but innocent notes and plot points that read like something out of an '80s slasher fan fiction.

"Of course not."

"Then you might want to go find her before George does. Or the killer," Jenna said, but Max was already rising to his feet.

"I know where she is. I just wasn't gonna send George her way. Keep that safe for me," he pointed to the journal and dusted off his pants. "I'll be back soon. If I'm not, come and find us at the lake."

Annie and Jenna came back to the kitchen, armed with their newfound knowledge. They discovered Vera, along with Hailey, Billy, and Ale, sitting with Neil, who was fast asleep. Vera appeared visibly stressed, frustrated, and tired. Interestingly, the three campers in the circle seemed to be the most composed.

"Now where is Max going?" Hailey asked.

"To get Jordan before George does," Annie replied.

"Good luck. That guy seems more motivated than any-one I've ever seen," Billy said. "Vera told us what hap-pened."

"So what should we do?" Ale asked. The campers looked at Annie for an answer, and she looked to Jenna because she was her senior.

"Don't look at me. I'm a couple of minutes away from taking a nap and just hoping it's all over by the time I wake up."

"That sounds like a great plan," Vera agreed, leaning back to lie on the floor, bundling her hair so that it would act as a pillow, then pulling down the bottom of her shirt that lifted above her navel during the motion.

"I just . . . I don't want to sit around," Annie said. "We have to help, somehow. Everyone is split up in the woods, and that's literally a step in Jordan's outline."

"*Outline*?" Vera asked. "That's what we're calling it? Not evil plan? Not manifesto?"

"I'm calling it an outline because it is one. George ig-nored the fucking title page and went straight to the text. She was getting ready to write a movie script," Annie ex-plained.

Vera sat up. "Seriously?"

"Yes, bitch," Jenna said, semi-jokingly. It sounded funny coming from her soft voice.

Vera tilted her head. "But if Jordan didn't do it, who did?"

"I'm sure we'll find out soon enough," Jenna predicted.

"I think we need to go after them," Annie proposed. "Find them, group up, and get everyone to one safe space."

"Go ahead. Count me out. "I'm comfortable right here." Vera lay back down again, this time without adjusting her top.

"I'll go with you." Billy offered.

"Me, too," Ale said.

"No, you guys stay here. It's my job to keep you safe, and I wouldn't be able to live with myself if I let something happen to either of you. Besides, Billy, I need you here to watch over the other campers. Especially Ale."

"My hero," Ale joked.

"Understood," Billy said.

"I'll go with you, then." Jenna volunteered.

"Thank you. Let's hurry," Annie urged. "If anything happens, ring the bell."

Billy smiled and said, "Yes, ma'am."

Chapter 21

Maybe this wasn't a great idea, Jordan thought as she stood naked on the pier, looking down at her reflection in the moonlit lake. *But while I'm in a daring mood, why not?* She dove into the ice-cold water and immediately regretted her decision, the lake stinging every nerve across her body.

They never addressed this problem in Friday the 13th, she thought as she swam back to the surface, squealing out a painful moan when she emerged. She brushed her hair out of her face, swinging it over her head to her back. When she opened her eyes to wet and distorted vision, she thought she saw a figure standing by the pier.

"Max? I thought you didn't want to come out tonight." She rubbed the water from her eyes and blinked three times, opening them again to see that nobody was there—at least, not anymore. "You know you don't have to hide, right? It would be a lot more fun if you joined me." The idea of seducing Max gave her newfound excitement.

"Unless voyeurism's your thing . . ." She lifted her legs to float on her back.

Loving the idea, she played along, swimming around in a flirtatious manner, pretending she was in a nude photoshoot, doing the backstroke, attempting an underwater handstand, etc.

She was having a lot of fun with it until a thought popped into her head. *What if it's not Max watching me?*

"Okay, Max, fun's over! Please come in and join me."

But if it isn't Max, who is it? Her mind raced. It could be anyone, from another counselor like George (which she wouldn't mind that much) or Neil (which would absolutely disgust her)

to Mitch or even a camper.

"Max? Seriously, you're scaring me," she yelled when he didn't respond. "You're making me look like the dumb girl in a slasher movie right now, and I do not want to be that girl, regardless of how much I love those movies." She scanned the trees, hoping to spot some sort of movement, but as far as she could tell, she was alone.

Did I imagine it?

"Okay, you lost your chance! Sorry, not sorry." Having officially freaked herself out, she swam back to the pier. She placed her palms on the wooden planks and used all her strength to lift her torso above the lake, then the water beneath her made an odd sound. It sounded like somebody else came out of the water with her. Still holding herself up with the assistance of the pier, she tried to look over her shoulder to see if someone was behind her, but she lost her balance and slipped, falling back into the water. She hurried to the surface and just as she emerged, she felt her lower half go numb following a loud *crack*. She couldn't feel her legs while she tried kicking them to stay afloat, yet she remained suspended above the lake.

She glanced down and noticed an unsettling movement in the flesh between her breasts. It seemed as though something inside her was desperately trying to break free. Frozen with fear, she witnessed her chest slowly opening up. Warm, slippery blood trickled down her stomach, accompanied by an intense pressure emanating from her back. Suddenly, her chest split wide open with a spraying gush of blood. The sight was gruesome, yet amidst the haze of her thoughts, she couldn't help but marvel at how this scene would have been perfect for a movie. Her memory faded soon after, but she distinctly recalled the sound of Max's piercing scream before everything went dark.

"Wake up!" Max said, shaking Jordan's body after dragging it out of the lake. He had been trained and certified in CPR as a Camp Safe Woods requirement, but he could not perform it on her because the machete that impaled her still rested perfectly centered, entering through her back and emerging from her chest, blocking the area for compressions.

Her body felt weak and limp in his arms, bringing back Max's most painful memories from the night he spent in the slaughterhouse all those years ago. Her extra-pale skin had been stained crimson from the blood spilled in a pattern that mirrored the tears streaming down his face.

"Not like this, Jordan! Wake up!" He knew it wouldn't help, but he tried performing mouth-to-mouth anyway—anything to make her conscious. He held her nose, pressed his lips to hers and breathed into her, repeating the process three times before looking at her closed eyes and seeing the face of the girl he gave himself to less than an hour earlier a hundred yards from where they were now. He felt helpless trying to save her, but he wouldn't give up. "Wait here, I'm gonna go get help. You're gonna get through this, I promise." As soon as the words left his mouth, a drip of water landed on her forehead.

He wiped away the tears on his cheeks, but more drips followed, landing on Jordan and Max and the dirt surrounding them. Max looked up for the first time since finding her injured and rainwater poured down on him.

Of course, he thought.

Not knowing how to position her on the ground without getting in the way of the machete, he gently rolled her on her side and stood up, dusting off his jeans—a force of habit. He hesitated to leave, fearing he might never see Jordan alive again if he did, but ultimately concluded he had no other choice. With that, he sprinted into the woods.

"Help!" he yelled, his voice seemingly quiet beneath the pouring rain that now enveloped the woods and camp. "Anybody, help!" Running at full speed, he lost his footing on some mud, planted his lead leg to regain his balance, and tripped on something, sending him face-first to the forest floor. Rather than wiping the mud away, he focused on getting back on track and finding help. He tried using his hands to push himself up, but whatever he had tripped on was now wrapped around his ankle. He tried pulling his leg out of it, but it pulled back and lifted him off the ground, suspending him in midair upside down.

"What the—" He looked at the rope contraption and realized that he must've triggered a trip wire disguised in the dirt, then immediately thought back to Ale, who stepped on a trap of her own the day before.

He struggled, kicking his leg in an attempt to fall out of it, but it wouldn't budge. He tried reaching for it with his hands, but it was too far out of reach—his abdominal muscles weren't strong enough to lift him. "Somebody help me!"

He heard footsteps nearby, snapping twigs and squishing mud. He struggled to look behind him as the blood rushing to his head made him feel dizzy, and his angle wasn't great to begin with. "Is somebody there?"

"Max?"

"You've gotta be kidding me," George said as soon as the first raindrop fell on him. He was already cold enough out in these dark woods well past midnight. On top of that, he had already done a lap around the camp, searching every cabin and bathroom he could think of but didn't find any clue as to Jordan's whereabouts. Still, with a killer lurking about the camp, he didn't care what kind of adversity he had to go through to put an end to it. A little bit of rain was certainly not enough to stop him. Not while there was a risk of more people getting hurt.

And while the darkness was easy enough to navigate through the camp with the occasional lamp lighting up the walkways, he knew his next search target was a short distance through the woods to the lake, and it wasn't a walk he was comfortable making without a flashlight. Luckily for him, he finished his lap near the counselors' cabin, where he not only had a flashlight waiting for him in his bag, but a jacket to help him weather the storm.

He entered the cabin and flicked the light switch, then walked to the dresser against the wall, opened the drawer filled with his belongings, pulled out his backpack, and grabbed the flashlight. He tested it first—pressing the rubber button on its shaft while foolishly looking directly into it and leaving himself temporarily blinded.

"Damn," he said, rubbing his eyes. "I guess it doesn't need batteries." He stood the flashlight upright atop the dresser and went back into his drawer to find his puffy rain jacket. When he pulled it out, a sleeve got caught beneath his backpack. He roughly yanked it out, causing the caught sleeve to slingshot out, whip the flashlight, and knock it over. "Shit!"

It landed on its side and rolled off the dresser. George tried to catch it as it fell, but he missed. It hit the floor with a loud *thud*, and he watched it continue rolling across the cabin until it was beneath the bunk bed in the nearest corner.

With a sigh, he acknowledged his unfortunate situation and placed his jacket neatly on the dresser. Slowly, he made his way toward the bed and positioned himself on his stomach to maneuver underneath it. The flashlight had rolled all the way to the farthest corner, just out of his reach. Determined, he inched forward, squeezing his broad shoulders tightly beneath the bed frame. Stretching his arm out, he reached as far as he could until his fingertips finally brushed against the flashlight, barely touching it.

"There you are, almost got it," he said, and using the tips of his fingers he rolled the flashlight closer to him and finally grabbed it. He let out a sigh of relief just as he felt a terrible stabbing pain in his lower back. "AGH!" he screamed, and three more quick jabs stabbed into him. He realized it was the killer behind him, taking advantage of his compromising position to attack.

The unidentified attacker forcefully seized hold of George's ankles and yanked him out from under the bed. He attempted to turn his head to catch a glimpse of the assailant, but his stab wounds hindered any swift movement. In a brutal act, the assailant stomped on George's head, forcefully driving his face onto the floor and leaving him dazed. This provided enough time to tightly cover George's head with a pillowcase and press one hand firmly against his mouth and nose, effectively suffocating him.

George did what he could and bit their hand, but they didn't pull away. He tried to punch them but they sat in an awkward position on his back, so George couldn't land a good hit without injuring himself even more. He felt his breath escaping his body until there was none left.

"What the hell happened?" Annie asked Max, suspended in the air and soaking wet. His face had turned red. She looked at Jenna to confirm that they were both seeing the same thing as they ran to his aid.

"Thank God it's you guys," he said, temporarily relieved. "Jordan, she—"

"Did you find her?" Jenna interrupted, as she and Annie fiddled with the rope around his ankle. The water had swelled the material, leaving the knot tighter and more difficult to undo.

"She's dead."

Both girls let go of the rope and looked at him, lost for words.

"I found her by the lake, impaled by a fucking machete." He sounded like he was crying, but Annie couldn't say for sure, given the rainwater streaming down his face.

"No . . . There's no way." Jenna started crying herself, and not just because she lost a friend. She was terrified. They all were. And while Annie was also scared, she could tell by the looks on their faces that they were going through something she would never understand. Jenna was shaking at the knees, and not because she was cold. Max would do the same if his knees weren't over his head right now. "Not Jordan." Her voice cracked when she spoke.

"I was on my way back to the cafeteria to get help and got caught in this trap." He motioned his hands to the rope. Annie snapped back into the moment and tried untying him once again, but her hands burned and kept slipping. "Please, just . . . get me out of this."

"I can't," Annie said, pulling at the rope as hard as she could. Her hand slipped and flew backward, punching herself in the cheek. She could feel the bruise immediately. "We need something to cut you down . . ." she said, trailing off as she started thinking to herself, *Did he mention a machete by the lake?*

She brushed the thought away almost as soon as it arrived. He said it impaled her. They were in an urgent situation, but not urgent enough to pull a blade from her friend's corpse to cut this rope. They would have to find something else.

"Jenna," Annie said, snapping her friend back to reality. "We need to find something to cut him down, and we need to do it quickly."

Jenna nodded. "Okay. Our cabin is probably the closest place with a knife."

"You can't just leave me alone!" Max yelled. "Can't one of you stay? I'm completely helpless here." He kicked his leg, hoping to slip out from the rope.

"We'll be much quicker if we go together. The faster we get you down, the better. Besides, if one of us goes off on our own and has a run-in with the killer, you'll still be stuck and unaware that help won't come," Annie said, to Max's dismay.

"Just be quick." He tried reaching up for the knot, struggled, and fell back to his hanging position, defeated.

Annie and Jenna proceeded through the forest, doing their best not to slip on the mud that kept sliding beneath them. Annie couldn't help but feel the gloom emanating from Jenna during their awkward, silent jog.

"I'm sorry about Jordan," Annie said, fighting the breaths that fell out of her with every heavy step.

"I just don't believe it," Jenna said. "I can't believe it."

"Do you think Max is lying?" Annie asked. They were approaching the cabin.

"No . . . Well, not exactly. He wouldn't have hung himself like that on purpose. And if it was his trap and he hung himself by accident, then that would mean he's the killer, and I don't want to believe that either." She stopped in front of the door.

"After we cut him down, we can look for her body. If .. . You know. If it would help."

"Absolutely not. I've seen enough corpses in my life. I'll die before I see another one."

Annie twisted the knob, opened the door, and turned on the light. Jenna screamed, drawing Annie's attention away for just a second, and when she looked back, she saw what frightened her. They were looking at George's limp body, his torso hanging off the edge of his top bunk and a trail of blood running down his face, dripping to the floor from unseen wounds; displayed as though his killer wanted to strike the highest amount of fear in whoever found him.

Without much thinking, Annie wanted to check and see if he was okay, so she ran to him.

"Quick, get in here!" Annie yelled, reaching to feel George's neck for a pulse. She wasn't sure if she was checking right, but it was what people did in the movies. She felt nothing until a blunt object smashed against her temple, sending her crashing to the floor.

Her mind felt hazy as she lay on her side, gazing out toward the doorway. She found herself seeing two Jennas, both in identical positions standing at the entrance, their hands clasped over their mouths as they screamed. Gradually, the two Jennas merged in her vision, blending into a single blurred figure, while a shadowy silhouette emerged from behind Annie. Recognition dawned on Jenna as she realized who it was.

"It was you?" Jenna's lower jaw quivered as the words left her mouth. She turned and bolted for the forest, and the figure followed her as Annie's eyes fell shut.

Chapter 22

This can't be happening, Vera thought. She pinched her arm and winced at the pain but didn't wake up. She brought her hand up and smacked herself across the face, hard. Then she looked up at the confused campers who stared at her judgmentally just as the door for the cafeteria opened, drawing their attention away from her and to the cold air and heavy pouring rain.

Nick stepped inside, rubbing his arms and shaking the water from his hair. He was completely soaked. He looked around the cafeteria as he approached Vera, who sat in the corner by herself.

"Where is everyone?" he asked.

Vera shrugged her shoulders. "Looking for you, I guess. Neil went to the bathroom like twenty minutes ago."

Nick nodded, but it didn't seem like he was really listening. He seemed more focused on Vera's face. "Look at me," he said, pulling her chin up by his index finger, then brushing her hair out of her face and exposing the fresh red mark she left on her cheek. "What happened?"

"I'm not handling tonight too well." Her voice broke with her words.

He sighed and pulled his hand away. "Come on." He stood up and offered his hand. She took it and followed him to the kitchen, where he took a seat on the floor beneath the refrigerator.

"What are we doing?" Vera asked.

"Getting away from the campers. You look like you need to talk, so I figured some privacy would be nice."

"Talking about tonight is the last thing I want to do," she said, pacing back and forth in front of the stove.

"So let's not. Let's talk about something else."

"Like what?"

"Whatever would make a good distracting conversation to take our minds off of everything else that's happening," he said. Vera stopped pacing and waited for him to say something, which he did. "Do you remember your first year at camp?"

"Of course," she said.

"I remember seeing you when you got off the bus."

"You do?" Vera took a seat beside him.

"Yeah." He chuckled and smiled. "I basically ran up to you and offered to help with your bags."

"No, you didn't! That asshole Alex Garcia took my bags."

"You're not remembering it correctly. I did come up to you, but you were so smitten with him that you ignored me and asked him to do it."

"Really? I didn't even see you," she said, and he laughed. "But to be fair, he was really cute."

"So what makes you call him an asshole?"

"What, you don't think he was?"

"Well, I do, sure. But I want to hear your reason."

"I didn't like the way he talked to me. He would treat me like I wasn't traumatized enough because he had seen more death than anyone else at the camp. It was like he thought he was special for surviving his traumatic event, and the rest of us hadn't undergone the same."

Nick laughed.

"You think that's funny?"

"No, no . . . You painted a great picture of him. Just imagine how he treated me. He even gave me the nickname, 'The Death Virgin.'"

Vera laughed. "I remember that. I always thought it was kinda funny."

Nick smiled and waited for her laughing to stop before he continued. "Do you remember when I asked you out?"

Her eyes widened at being caught off guard. "I think so. That was during my second year at camp, right?"

"Yeah, it was."

"Don't tell me you're upset about that after all these years."

"No, of course not. It's not like you ever gave me an answer anyway. You just said, 'Let me think about it,' and we never spoke of it again. But at least I took the hint and moved on."

"Maybe that's for the best. I mean, look at Casey and Max! Camp romances never work out, and I'm not a long-distance relationship type of girl," she said.

"No, of course not."

Vera looked him up and down. "You look so much different now than you did back then, though. You were such a scrawny little nerd." She felt his bicep. "Now you're all fit. Maybe I would've looked at you differently then if you looked like you do now. Who knows?"

"Is that right?"

"Like I said, who knows?" She leaned over and whispered in his ear, "And who knows what would happen if you asked me out again after this is all said and done?" She watched the goose bumps crawl up his arm when she pulled away, then smiled.

"Is flirting how you usually calm yourself down?" he asked softly.

"It helps," she said, a bit confused at his response. She was used to men trembling when she came on to them.

"I guess that explains a lot."

"What's that supposed to mean?"

"Oh, nothing. I wanted to ask you another question, though."

"What's that?"

"When you told the camp your story last night, I couldn't help but notice that you didn't tell anyone who it was that attacked you and your friends. Why not?"

"I don't understand. How is that important?"

"Whenever a bunch of people die, isn't the only question people want answered, 'Who did it?'"

"Well, yeah, but . . . I don't see why you're bringing that up right now." Vera shifted in her seat on the floor. She started feeling uncomfortable.

"Call me curious," he said.

"Like I said last night, it was just some lunatic."

"That's it? Just somebody completely random walked into your house and cut up your friends?"

"It wasn't random." She looked down at the floor between her legs. "He was . . . He was our soccer coach. He had a psychotic break, followed us girls to my house, spied on us for his high school girl fetish, and eventually broke in and did what he did."

"He wasn't just your soccer coach, though, was he?"

"What are you implying?"

"Oh, I'm not implying anything. We both know there's a little more depth to that story of yours."

"Fuck you. You don't know anything."

"Yeah, I do. I don't know if you ever realized this, but I actually liked you quite a lot," he said. "So much so that I couldn't stop thinking about you."

Vera felt her confusion growing.

Nick continued. "I went online one year after camp finished and looked up your name—trying to find you on social media—but all that popped up were articles relating to that incident. Naturally, I clicked on a few of them."

"Okay, you were stalking me online? So what?"

"Admit it."

"Admit what?"

"You know what. Stop lying to people about who it was that hurt you and tell the truth."

Vera stood up, and Nick did the same.

"Seriously, who gives a fuck? Sure, my dad was the lunatic in my story. He was the soccer coach who jerked off outside my bedroom window while us girls gossiped in our pajamas. And no, he didn't need to break into the house because it was *his* house. What is your fucking point?"

"It must feel nice."

Vera looked at him like she was waiting for him to add context.

"Telling the truth about what happened," he said. "I can only imagine what that must feel like." Then he raised his shirt and pulled out the knife he had tucked away.

"I hope Annie is okay." Hailey sat with her friends at a table in the cafeteria, keeping an eye on the other campers since all the counselors had left them alone up to this point.

"Me, too," Billy said.

"What do you think they're doing?" Ale asked. Hailey and Billy looked at her. "Nick and Vera."

"She was in a pretty bummy mood. He's probably trying to cheer her up. That's kind of his job, even though she's a counsel—" Billy said, only to be interrupted by the kitchen door bursting open.

Every camper in the room instinctively turned their heads toward the sound. Amidst the chaotic screams of those around her, Hailey found herself enveloped in an eerie silence. Her attention was drawn to Nick, who stood over Vera's lifeless body, his hands stained with blood and a vacant, almost hostile expression on his face. Something about him seemed altered, but Hailey couldn't quite pinpoint what it was. It wasn't until he lifted his gaze from Vera and locked eyes with Hailey that she knew for certain—he killed her.

Alejandra pulled her arm and simultaneously pulled her back into the moment, then Hailey heard the screaming around her. "We need to go," Ale yelled, her arm around Billy's shoulder.

"Now!" Billy yelled at Hailey, who still wasn't moving. Nick bent down and ripped the knife that Hailey hadn't yet seen from the side of Vera's throat, and he started walking toward Hailey. Ale tugged on her arm again, and Hailey joined them in running out of the cafeteria at as fast a pace as they could without letting Ale trip.

When they got outside, Billy unwrapped Ale's arm from around his shoulder and shouted, "Keep running!" He stepped away from them and sprinted ahead.

"What the fuck are you doing?" Ale yelled to him while they fell sluggishly behind.

Would Billy really leave us? Hailey wondered. She turned and whispered, "Oh shit," at the sight of Nick emerging from the cafeteria doorway. He took a step toward them, then stopped at the unwelcome sound of the camp's morning bell. He looked distracted as he looked back into the cafeteria window before stepping back inside.

Hailey and Ale caught up to Billy at the bell, who pulled the string frantically until Ale hit his arm.

"That bell's fucking annoying," she said.

"I was trying to alert the counselors. You didn't have to hit me."

"They're alerted." She hit him again.

"Ouch!" he said, rubbing the red spot on his forearm.

"That's for leaving us behind," she said.

"I didn't! Besides,"—Billy pointed at the cafeteria—"it looks like it scared him away."

"Somehow I doubt that," Hailey said. "Let's get out of here while he can't see us."

"Where are we gonna go?" Ale asked.

Hailey shrugged her shoulders. "Hide in the woods, I guess. Waiting this one out might be our best option."

"I agree." Billy nodded and led the way.

Upon returning from the bathroom, Neil was greeted with nothing but confusion because the cafeteria was empty.

"Hello?" He yawned. He heard a scream from a camper outside, and then another. "I guess I'm not going out there," he said. He looked around the room for a place to hide and saw that the kitchen door was open.

Perfect, he thought. He walked at first, but the morning bell ringing outside frightened him, so he ran as fast as he could for the kitchen and tripped just as he tried to step around the door, falling face-first to the wooden floor. He hurried to the backside, looked across from him, and saw that he had tripped over Vera. A very dead Vera.

Too out of breath from running to scream, he shot his gaze to the doorway as Nick stepped inside. "Oh, Nick! I think the killer's here, and they got Vera!" he said as Nick approached with a knife in his right hand.

He only realized what was happening when Nick replied, "You don't say?" and raised the knife. As he brought it down, Neil flinched and tried to block it, bringing his hands up and in front of his face. The knife pierced straight through his palm, cracking the bones inside and ripping through his skin. He stared in awe as a small trail of blood poured from the wound and down his hand, until Nick pulled the knife out and the small trail became a spouting geyser, raining red onto his face.

Nick continued his attack, but Neil had no more fight in him. The final thrust split through the bridge of his glasses before crashing through his skull and piercing his brain.

*T*hump *thump.*

Thump thump.

Shivering cold, soaking wet, a gut-wrenching fear that rivaled Halloween night all those years ago, and yet all Max could focus on was the pounding sensation of blood pumping in his head from being suspended upside down for so long.

How long had it been? he wondered. It felt like hours since Jenna and Annie had left him hanging, but in reality, it hadn't even been a half hour yet. Time moved so slowly trapped in a situation like this, with nothing but the image of his dead friend terrorizing his every thought—a friend with whom he had just formed a much deeper connection. A connection he had every intention of pursuing, developing, and deepening.

When he saw the shadowy figure approaching from the woods, his first thought was, *Why aren't there two?* It was both Annie and Jenna who ran off to look for help, and if one of them could return without the other now, then why couldn't one of them have stayed behind with him while he was stuck here?

As the person got closer, he could tell that it wasn't a feminine figure approaching, and he feared the worst: the killer whose trap had caught him was en route to claim their victim.

"Wow, Max," they said. A familiar voice. Especially once he recognized the camp counselor uniform they were wearing, then even more so when he saw it was none other than the head counselor himself: Nick. And for the final bit of relief, he was holding a kitchen knife Max recognized as one from their cabin. "Looks like you've got yourself in quite a pickle."

"Did the girls send you?" Max asked.

"Girls?"

"Yeah, Jenna and Annie. They left me here a while ago to find something to cut me down."

"Oh yeah, I ran into them at the cabin," Nick said. He tapped the knife against his temple. "I would've gotten here a lot sooner if they had told me you were trapped."

"They didn't tell you?" Max asked. He felt as though being held upside down for this long, his brain had malfunctioned. Why was Nick here with a knife if they didn't tell him? It didn't make sense, so surely he had misheard him, right? Or was he just hallucinating, and Nick wasn't really here after all?

"No. They didn't." He started walking in a circle around Max, as if admiring the predicament he was in. "You ought to be more careful. After that camper tripped over the bear trap, it's hard to imagine someone actually falling for another one. I mean, how stupid can you be?"

"Nick, quit playing around. This is serious shit. Jordan's dead. Or she's dying, and we need to get her help. We need to find somebody before we can't save her, and I've been stuck here for too long."

Nick laughed. "So you found her, huh? Sorry to say it, but she's definitely dead."

"What are you—"

"She was calling for you before it happened. The dumb bitch was skinny-dipping and thought you were going to join her." He chuckled. "Perhaps things would've been much better for you if you had."

"You . . .?"

"I mean, those chances aren't high, though. What would two naked idiots have been able to do to somebody with a machete? At least you could've died together. That would've been more beautiful and poetic. Instead, she had to die alone and scared, and you get to die hung like a pig in a slaughterhouse." Nick stopped and thought about his words. "Now that I think about it, considering your history, I guess it is poetic after all."

Nick thrust his knife into the base of Max's neck. He tried to scream, but all that came out was a gurgling mess as his mouth filled with the taste of pennies. He felt the burn of a slash across his stomach, followed by one final slash across his throat. As his eyes were stained with blood and his consciousness faded, the last vision he had before his mind went blank was of Jordan's smile in the storage shed. That memory filled his body with enough warmth for him to pass peacefully.

Chapter 23

Warmth, Annie thought. As the tingling sensation burned through her bladder, she woke to an equally warm sensation gracing her body. With the orange tint illuminating her closed eyelids and the crackling sound of a fire, Annie remembered she was at Camp Safe Woods, and she convinced herself she must've fallen asleep during that night's campfire. And the nightmare that followed was simply that—a nightmare.

As the cold breeze cut through the air, Annie shivered and felt the dampness seep into her clothes. Her head throbbed relentlessly and her body ached in unfamiliar places. The sound of her own labored breathing filled her ears, echoing her exhaustion. The scent of damp earth mingled with the mustiness of her surroundings, intensifying her discomfort. Determined to resist the temptation of sleep, she summoned the strength to pry her heavy eyelids open.

First, she noticed that this wasn't the same campfire located at the center of Camp Safe Woods. This one was makeshift, dug in a shallow pit in the mud. Sitting around the fire were just two familiar faces: Jenna and Mitch. She blinked a few times, clearing the fog in her eyes enough to see their distressed state.

Both of them, like Annie, were soaking wet. Mitch's face and hands were covered in mud, and she noticed various cuts along his arms, staining his shirt red. Mitch was seated in and tied to a plastic folding chair. Jenna had it much worse. She was lying on her back in the mud, her hands tied behind her back and her feet tied together. Her Camp Safe Woods T-shirt was cut open straight down the middle, blood staining her torso and bra from an unseen cut beneath the cruor. Her hair was wet, matted, and muddy. Her skin was pale and bruised all over. With both of them, at the very least, unconscious, Annie wasn't sure whether or not they were still alive.

She made an attempt to stand and approach them, but her feet and arms were securely tied to a chair. She stumbled and fell face-first onto the muddy ground, the chair still tightly bound to her back. Frustration and fear overwhelmed her, but she took a deep breath and concentrated.

What do I do? The sounds of campers screaming in the distance interrupted her thought process. *What can I do?*

With no other options, she joined them in screaming for help.

"I can't believe it was Nick," Hailey said, as they trudged through the forest unsure of where they were going, aside from the opposite direction of the camp.

"I can," Ale said. "You have to admit, it's a little weird that he is so fond of this camp, considering he's never suffered the trauma you guys have. He probably just wanted to get in on the action."

"That's sickening." Billy shook his head. "What we've been through . . . that's nothing to wish upon anybody."

Hailey nodded in agreement, unsure of what else she could say. Nick had been nothing but nice since they'd met. How could it be that someone with such an energetic and positive personality had such a twisted side to them?

"Hey, do you see that up there?" Ale asked. She pointed to what looked like a silver sedan parked between some trees.

Hailey squinted. "Is that a car?"

"I think so. And it looks like its tires haven't been popped yet," Billy said.

"Who do you think it belongs to?" Ale asked.

"Only one way to find out." Billy led them to the vehicle, and as they approached, a rancid scent filled the forest.

The windows were all fogged up, yet the driver's window was slightly cracked. Billy peeked inside.

"Do you see anything?" Hailey asked.

"I'm not sure. It's so dark in there."

"Some keys, maybe?" Ale hoped.

"Not from here, at least. Wait, I think I see blood."

"What? Where?" Hailey asked, peering inside herself.

"On the back door handle."

Hailey looked, and there it was, splattered across the door and the back seat. Below that was what looked like a body.

She took a step back, and Billy realized she was scared. "What did you see?"

"On the floor in the back. Is that—"

Billy looked and confirmed. "Oh no." He pulled the door handle, but it was locked. He tried the back door, also locked. He took a deep breath and crashed his elbow into the window, expecting it to shatter like he had seen in the movies, but there was only a muffled *thud* followed by his pain-filled groan.

Ale, who had limped her way to the other side of the sedan, tried the handle on the passenger door, and it opened. She laughed at Billy, then stopped as soon as the wave of putrid smells hit her, and she gagged. "I'm gonna puke."

Billy and Hailey rushed to her side, where Hailey helped walk her away from the car, and Billy pushed the button to unlock all the doors. He opened the rear one with the bloodstained handle. "Jesus," he said, disgust in his voice.

Hailey and Ale both turned to look and saw the source of the odor and blood—Betty's corpse, which had been dumped and left to rot in this car.

"Is she dead?" Ale asked. Billy and Hailey looked at her like she was stupid.

"Yes. Very," Billy said. The obvious cause of death was the barbecue fork stabbed through the center of her forehead.

"Hey, don't look at me like that. You guys are the mass murder veterans, not me," Ale said.

"Welcome to the club," Hailey said, following Billy to the trunk of the car. He placed one hand on the <**TRUNK RELEASE**> button and used the other to cover his nose. Hailey thought it was a good idea and did the same in case there was another body waiting for them.

Fortunately, there was not. The contents inside consisted of a wide array of items one might typically discover in the closet of a serial killer's residence: ropes, duct tape, a crossbow, garbage bags, knives of different sizes, and another bear trap that looked exactly like the one Ale had stumbled upon earlier. What held the greatest significance for them was the open garbage bag brimming with all the cell phones belonging to the campers and counselors.

"So this is where he hid them?" Ale asked.

"I guess so." Billy began picking through the bag, holding the power buttons on all the phones, hoping for one to turn on, but they all seemed to be dead.

"Did he drain all the batteries?" Hailey asked, grabbing one from the bag herself and trying it.

"Seems so," Billy said, frustrated.

"Wait," Hailey said as the phone in her hand illuminated. "Aha!"

"You got one?" Ale asked, looking over her shoulder.

When the phone finished turning on, they were greeted with a lock screen featuring a selfie of Jordan winking at the camera and holding a machete in a Jason Voorhees costume with the hockey mask pulled back over the top of her head.

"Is that the counselor?"

"Yeah," Hailey said, swiping to unlock the phone, but it was requesting a PIN. She sighed. "Any guesses?"

"No, I didn't know her like that," Billy said.

"She's wearing a Halloween costume on her lock screen picture. Try 1031," Ale suggested.

"Oh, good idea." Hailey typed in the code, but it didn't work.

"Here, lemme see." Billy reached for the phone and she gave it to him. "Most phones nowadays let you make emergency calls without unlocking them." He pressed the screen a few times and said, "There we go." He held the phone up to his ear and stepped away from them while he made the call.

"Hello? Yeah, hi. My name's Billy and I'm here at Camp Safe Woods. Yeah . . . You know where that is? Okay, good. I need you to send the police and several ambulances. Multiple murders have taken place here tonight. At least two, and maybe more. Yeah, it was the head counselor here. His name is Nick . . . I don't recall his last name. Please, just send help." Billy paused and listened to the emergency services dispatcher. "Thank you." He hung up the phone.

"Well, what did they say?" Ale asked.

"Are they sending help?" Hailey crossed her fingers.

"Yeah, but it could take a while. She reminded me we aren't exactly close to any police stations."

"So what do we do in the meantime?" Ale asked.

"Wait until they get here," Billy said.

Hailey shook her head. "No. We can't."

Ale looked at her wide-eyed. "What do you mean, 'We can't'?"

"If we just wait around, Nick can attack us at any moment. Or he's out there killing other people and I don't feel comfortable letting him do that. Like, what about Annie? George? The others? If we have a chance to do something about it, I think we should," Hailey asserted.

"And what do you think we should do? I'm not sure if you noticed, but I'm sort of crippled here."

"If you want to wait around, I don't blame you. Billy might even be able to protect you, but I'm gonna go look for other people. Maybe gather a group to find Nick and put a stop to this."

"You mean kill him?" Ale asked.

"It wouldn't sound so bad if you go look at what he did to Betty in the car over there," Hailey said. "But I'm gonna take a knife from the trunk and go see what happens. Feel free to join me."

"Help isn't coming, dear." Nick's voice came from behind Annie.

"Nick? Is that you?" she asked, trying to turn her head, but it was no use.

"Who else?" He lifted Annie's chair to its vertical position. She tried to kick her legs free, but the knot was far too tight—her feet had even numbed from the loss of blood flow. Once she was righted, Nick walked to the other side of the fire. He held a long knife dripping blood. "All the other counselors are either . . ." He pointed at Jenna and said, "Well, here . . . or dead."

"No. I don't believe you."

He held up the knife, brandishing it to make sure she saw the spattered blood across the blade. "Is this not proof enough? I mean, you saw George yourself. Did you think I would have trouble with anyone else? Neil couldn't outrun a turtle, and Vera probably only weighs double digits."

"No . . . Not them," Annie lamented, speaking more to herself than to Nick. "How could you do something like that?"

"It was actually quite easy." He walked to Mitch as he said, "And it's all thanks to your grandfather here offering me the head counselor position."

Annie screamed as Nick raised the knife above Mitch, only to bring it down handle-first onto the back of his head. Mitch grunted and looked up. Annie's scream must've woken Jenna, too, as she started coughing before pulling at the ropes that bound her.

"Nick?" Mitch asked, confused as Nick stepped in front of him, knife in hand.

"What the—" Jenna muttered, before screaming, "Help!" at the top of her lungs.

"Jenna, Jenna, it's okay," Annie said, drawing Jenna's eyes to hers. "It's gonna be okay." She spoke the words, even though she wasn't so sure. Jenna didn't believe her, either, as she analyzed the ropes that held Annie to the chair.

"Nick, I don't understand what's going on," Mitch said. "I found Betty . . . She . . . That wasn't you, was it? Please tell me that wasn't you!"

"Quiet!" Nick yelled, stopping in front of a chair directly across the firepit from Annie. Everyone went silent and watched as he sat down and pulled a black backpack from beneath it.

"Nick, what are you—" Mitch tried to speak, but Nick raised his knife and pointed it his way without saying a word. Mitch understood and swallowed his words.

Nick brought the knife down, stabbing it into his backpack. When he pulled it out, he had skewered a marshmallow. He calmly scooted his chair closer to the fire and extended his arm to roast it.

"I want to tell you all a story."

"I don't want to hear it," Mitch said.

"I don't think you have much of a choice now, do you?" He laughed. "For years, I spent countless hours listening to every kid's sob story around the campfire." He stood up and yelled, "Now it's my turn!" He sat back down and twirled the knife in his hand.

"Your turn? Ha! Your turn for what?" Mitch chuckled. "Is that what this is? Have all these horror stories corrupted your brain? Or are you somehow jealous of what these poor kids have been through and made up a story of your own?"

"You see, it's that,"—Nick pointed his knife back at Mitch—"that right there! That is exactly why tonight is happening. But not just because you said it. No. Because I had to hear it from just about every camper and counselor I've come across at this fucking place. Day after day, year after year, everyone telling me how lucky I am to live this innocent, carefree, and traumaless life." He brought the marshmallow on his knife back over the flame and stared at the fire, as if watching a bad memory within it. "Meanwhile, I was the most unlucky of you all."

Annie and Mitch shared a confused look at each other, both of them now intently listening to Nick.

"While all of you had this community of peers to talk about your problems with, I had to listen to everyone tell me how lucky I was while I was forced to keep my problems to myself," Nick said, his marshmallow ablaze. He blew the flame out, then pulled it off the knife with his teeth. Annie gagged at the thought of the blood that undoubtedly seasoned the marshmallow.

"What are you talking about? If you had something you needed to talk about, you could've! That's the entire purpose of this place," Mitch said.

"No, you see,"—Nick swallowed the sticky bits he was still chewing on—"that's where you're wrong. I wasn't allowed to talk about it. But that all changes tonight."

"Just spit it out already," Annie said. Nick shot her a dirty I-wasn't-talking-to-you look, pointing the knife in her direction. Annie swallowed her fear and continued, saying, "If you want to tell your story so bad, do it."

"Very well, then." Nick cleared his throat. "Forgive me if you've heard this one already, but this story doesn't exactly end how everyone thinks it does."

Annie and Mitch shared another confused look, then she looked at Jenna, who she had avoided looking at as best as she could. Seeing her in the kind of pain she was in wasn't something Annie would ever forget. Her chest heaved at an insane pace and she gritted her teeth. Her eyes remained closed as she listened to Nick's ramble.

"Do you guys remember the story of Victoria Vance?"

"The girl who killed Woodsby's owner?" Annie asked, uncertain.

"Ding ding ding," Nick said, reaching into his backpack and pulling out a marshmallow. "Good job. Here's a reward." He threw the marshmallow at her underhanded, as if expecting her to catch it with her mouth. She made no such effort. It smacked her right breast and bounced onto the mud. Then he stabbed his knife into another marshmallow and rested it along the firepit to roast while he continued his story.

"If you remember the story as it's told, they say that she went house to house, killing everyone in their neighborhood, including her own family, until she eventually found her little brother, Oliver, and killed him too. That story is truthful, at least . . . until the ending. She never found her little brother." Nick stood up. "That night, I was having nightmares, you see. It must've been the screaming throughout the neighborhood creeping into my ears, but the point is, I couldn't sleep, so I thought it best to leave my friend's house early and head home. What I didn't know was that my sister was killing people in those very homes I walked past on my way there."

"So that means . . . you are Oliver Vance?" Mitch asked.

"In the flesh." Nick smiled and took a bow. "When I found my parents, what was left of them, I called the police. They came and searched the place, then quickly found more bodies in the neighboring houses and nearly caught my sister, but she got away."

"I-I just don't get it," Mitch stuttered. "Why didn't you tell me? You could've told me!"

"No, I couldn't have. Following the events of the murder, I was placed in witness protection. It wasn't supposed to be long-term, just long enough for them to catch Vicky. But to this day, she is out there, somewhere."

"It sounds to me like crazy runs in your blood, then," Annie said. At this point, she had given up on the idea of survival. If someone could come and save them, great. But if not, the least she could do was insult the lunatic seated before her.

"Crazy? Vicky, maybe. But not me. I'm not crazy, I am broken. True, the kids here have experienced pain, but not like me. I didn't just lose my friends and family. I lost my identity. Can you even imagine what that does to a person?" He laughed. "Well, I guess you can because you're seeing it now. But none of this is happening because I'm 'crazy.' This is all just one big plot of revenge."

"Revenge?" Jenna asked, fighting to even get the word out. "If you wanted revenge, you should've taken it on your sister."

"Yeah, not the people of this camp who've gone through enough," Mitch said.

"And I will, in time. After tonight, pictures of my face will be everywhere. Maybe she'll come out of hiding and try to face me again. But for now, I'm taking my revenge on everyone who told me I hadn't suffered enough, and on you, Mitch, for making a place like this—where, rather than helping a victim, you failed and created a monster."

"And what about Annie?" Mitch asked. "She's completely innocent in all of this."

Nick faced her and said, "Annie, he is right. So know that none of this is personal. You weren't supposed to be here. Consider your death a punishment for your grandfather's failures. And at least you won't have to live this fucked-up, traumatized life for as long as I have."

Chapter 24

The words sent cold shivers down Annie's spine. How could someone talk about her death so casually? She held her breath as Nick pulled another knife from his bag, leaving the other with the marshmallow still attached to roast as he approached her. Behind him, she spotted Hailey tiptoeing toward them from the forest, then reverted her eyes back to Nick, hoping he hadn't noticed that she saw someone. Unfortunately, he did.

As Hailey got closer, she charged at him, but he was prepared, turning around and swinging the knife as she tackled him.

"Hailey, no!" Annie yelled when Hailey rolled off of Nick, and she saw the handle of the knife sticking out of her side. Hailey gasped for air and her hands shivered as she tried moving them toward the knife, as if she were planning on pulling it out and using it.

Annie struggled in the chair, desperately attempting to reach Hailey. However, she only ended up toppling to the ground once more—this time, injuring her nose, causing tears to well up in her eyes. Summoning every ounce of strength from her abdomen, she managed to roll over, successfully tipping herself and the chair onto its side. This allowed her to regain sight of Hailey just as Billy emerged from the forest, screaming like a maniac. He swiftly tackled Nick, preventing him from standing.

Billy sat on Nick's ribs, punching him in the face, first one hand at a time, then bringing both hands down on him like a hammer. Meanwhile, Ale got behind Annie's chair and began cutting the ropes that tied her.

"The police are on their way," Ale whispered.

"You called them?"

"Uh-huh."

Fed up with the relentless beating, Nick extended his right arm toward Hailey, searching for the knife lodged in her torso. Meanwhile, Billy continued to pummel Nick's face. Upon locating his target, Nick swiftly yanked the knife out, slashing it across Billy's face in one swift motion. The blade sliced through his cheek, forming a wide gash that stretched from his jaw to his mouth, extending his smile. Billy recoiled in agony, shrieking and desperately clawing at the wound, as if attempting to mend the severed flesh.

"Billy!" Ale yelled as Annie felt the last cut free the ropes around her hands. Ale hastily limped to Billy's side and held his head to her chest, the wound spilling blood onto her shirt.

"Wait!" Annie yelled to her, assuming she'd realize that she had forgotten to cut off the ropes around her legs. But Ale didn't even look her way, so caught up with helping Billy. On her own, and with the freedom of her hands, she removed her shoes so she could slip her feet through the knot. As she struggled to stand, she watched Nick do the same, stabbing his knife into the ground and using it for leverage to push himself up, but he couldn't do it. His arms and legs trembled with every attempt and he repeatedly collapsed on the ground. Annie took the opportunity, ran to Jenna's side, and attempted to untie her.

"We're gonna make it through this," Annie promised, struggling with the rope just as much as they did with the one that trapped Max. "Ale, help!" she yelled, but she was far too focused on Billy than the situation at hand to hear her.

"Annie." Jenna raised a single finger to point at Nick, now standing, knife in hand, with a menacing shadow cast across his body as the flame danced beside him.

Annie stood up, making a silent promise to herself that she would untie Jenna as soon as the opportunity arose. As Nick took a step toward her, Annie stepped in the opposite direction, both circling around the fire at the same pace, watching each other like cats do before they strike.

Annie stopped circling when she felt her foot kick something. She quickly glanced down and saw the knife Nick had left behind—the marshmallow it skewered had a perfectly golden brown tip. She bent down to pick it up just as Nick charged her, and Hailey managed to crawl far enough to catch him by the ankle and send him falling face-first.

Annie grabbed the knife and brought it upward, jamming it into Nick's temple as he fell. Still holding the knife and Nick's body, she glared directly into his eyes as any thoughts left in his head escaped him. She shivered and tossed him aside, sending his body rolling into the campfire with the knife pointing straight up to the sky—skewering not only Nick but that perfectly golden brown marshmallow Nick's skull had pushed toward the hilt of the knife.

As the red and blue emergency lights illuminated the forest and the squirrel cabin's campers untied Mitch and Jenna, Annie watched as the marshmallow burned and melted, oozing over Nick's charred head. She said the only thing that came to mind, "I hate marshmallows."

Epilogue

*K**nock knock knock.*

Annie clutched the flowers tightly, her nerves getting the better of her as she gazed at the plain white hospital door. With a trembling hand, she turned the doorknob. On the other side, Woodsby let out a *woof.* The door creaked when she cautiously stepped inside. The hospital room appeared much darker compared to the well-lit hallway outside. The only source of illumination came from a lone desk lamp casting a soft glow on a small, white rolling table and a sad food tray. On it sat an unopened container of applesauce alongside an empty pudding cup with a white plastic spoon resting against the side.

Sitting on the hospital bed—one leg above the blanket, exhaustion in her eyes but a smile on her face while watching old cartoons on the silent TV in the room's corner—was Hailey, her stuffed Loch Ness monster, Lana, held tightly in her lap.

"Heeey, girl," Annie said, stepping into the room and closing the door quietly behind her.

Hailey turned toward her and smiled. "Hey. It's good to see you."

Annie grabbed the plastic chair from the corner and slid it over to the bedside. "You too."

"I'd give you a hug, but—" Hailey grabbed at her untied gown and pulled it forward, exposing her side where bandages covered a fresh surgery incision.

"Don't worry about it. Seeing that you're okay is good enough for me," Annie said. She reached over Hailey's bed and placed the bouquet neatly on the rolling table. Woodsby, who was playing security guard on the opposite, unseen side of Hailey's bed, woofed and stood up.

"Uh-oh." Hailey laughed, then winced and held her side as her abdomen contracting must've shot pain straight to her wound. "My little savior is here to protect me."

"Yeah, he is." Annie reached down to pet the corgi on the head. "After you had fainted, when they wheeled the stretcher into the ambulance, he jumped in and rode with you all the way here."

"Billy told me." Hailey looked at Woodsby. "Such a good boy."

"He's the best," Annie said, scratching under his chin, his hind leg kicking uncontrollably. "You've seen some shit, haven't you, boy?"

"More than any of us," Hailey said. She looked back at the TV and squeezed Lana.

When Woodsby decided he'd had enough attention, he returned to the other side of the bed to lie down. Annie took her seat in the chair. "So you saw your friends already?"

"I saw Billy, but Ale's mom wanted to get out of town as soon as possible, so she was gone before I could see her. She gave her number to Billy for me, and we've been texting."

"That's good. I need to get your number too. After you saved my life, I at least owe you the occasional phone call to check in every now and then."

"Of course, and I'll give you theirs," Hailey said, right before her phone lit up.

Annie laughed. "I'm sure it's the last thing on your mind right now, but my grandpa, Mitch, wanted me to offer you a job as a counselor next season."

Hailey snickered, then winced again. "Please, don't make me laugh."

"Sorry." Annie frowned, feeling genuinely sorry for her.

"Are they even gonna let him open the camp next year?"

Annie shrugged her shoulders. "I honestly don't know. Part of me thinks any sane parents wouldn't send their kids there, considering what happened."

"True."

"But then again, the kids who were there might need to go back now more than ever. One thing's for sure, he won't confiscate phones again."

"He should probably consider running background checks on everyone involved too."

Annie nodded.

"And what about you?" Hailey asked.

"He wants me to be head counselor."

"Will you?"

"I'm not sure. It's an enormous responsibility and not really a role I want to fill, considering who I'd be replacing."

"Hmm. I might take up that job offer if you were there, though. At least, that's the only way I'd really even consider it."

"I'll keep that in mind," Annie said.

"Do you have any news on Jordan?" Hailey asked.

Annie looked at her, head tilted.

"Billy told me she had gone into surgery, but they weren't sure if she was going to make it."

"She's still in surgery as we speak, but it's looking rough. They said if she does make it, she's going to be paralyzed, most likely for life."

"Oh my gosh, do you know what happened to her?" Hailey asked.

"Nick impaled her with a machete. It went straight through her spine and emerged here." Annie pointed at the spot in her chest, directly between her breasts.

Hailey took a deep breath. "She'll make it through. I believe in her."

"Yeah, she will. She's the toughest girl I've ever met. She'll be more focused on the kick-ass scar between her titties than her inability to walk."

Hailey let out a laugh that quickly transitioned into a painful moan. "Ow, okay, stop . . . stop."

"Sorry." Annie chuckled.

Hailey picked up the remote from the table and started clicking through the silent channels. "If laughing feels this bad, I need to watch something boring." She stopped when she got to the news station that featured an old picture of Nick below the headline "CAMP SAFE WOODS? THINK AGAIN."

"He was right," Annie said. Hailey waited for her to elaborate. "Before you guys came to my rescue, he said his face was gonna be everywhere after last night, and his sister would finally see him again. He was right."

"I'm more worried about me having to see his face all the time." Hailey shook in disgust and went back to changing the channel.

"Hand me your phone," Annie said. "I'm gonna put my number in."

Hailey reached over to the chair beneath the table, pulled her phone from the charger cord, unlocked it, and handed it to Annie.

As Annie entered the digits, a message popped up from Ale. *Am I gonna be fucked-up like you now?* Annie knew it was a joke, but she didn't think of it as funny, considering she and Ale were in similar boats that would take some getting used to. She finished saving her number in the phone, then handed it back before standing from her chair.

"There you go. I'm gonna let you get some rest," Annie said.

"You need to get some too. You look like you haven't slept since everything happened," Hailey said.

Annie laughed. "I haven't, and I will. There's a hotel near the hospital. Mitch and I are staying there for a few days. If you need anything, anything at all,"—Annie pointed at Hailey's phone—"you call me."

"I will."

"I mean it. And not just over the next few days. You are an official camper of the squirrel cabin, and even though my summer job as a counselor is over, I want all of my squirrel campers to know that they can talk to me or ask me for anything, whenever. Seriously."

"Thank you. That means a lot."

"I hope so. If you want to hang out, just need someone to talk to, need boy advice, or need a recipe . . . I'm not a good cook, but I can learn if I need to. Come to think of it, I'm not great with boys either . . . But I can share opinions!"

Hailey gave a painful smile, trying not to laugh.

"Give my number to the others too. Let them know this offer extends to them."

"Of course. I promise," Hailey said.

"We're an exclusive club now." Annie stepped toward the door and tried thinking of a clever name for the four of them. "I'd call us 'The Final Girls,' but I'm not so sure Billy would approve."

"I've got it!" Hailey waved her hand, holding her index fingers and thumbs apart, framing her words, "The Slasher Victims."

Acknowledgements

This book is a culmination of my over decade long obsession with horror films—more specifically, slashers. As such, it takes *heavy* inspiration from these films, and might even make direct reference to a few. Since this book wouldn't exist without them, I wouldn't feel comfortable releasing this without thanking the following films/franchises:

Scream

Halloween

Friday the 13th

A Nightmare on Elm Street

X

Sleepaway Camp

Slumber Party Massacre

Child's Play

If I'm forgetting any, I'm sorry. There's far too many to name. Without the countless hours I've spent watching these films, this book simply wouldn't be here, so thank you.

Next up, I want to thank my lovely wife who is currently carrying my first child. Watching our family grow, and looking to our future is only inspiring me to do better in every avenue of life, and that includes becoming a better writer. Without your support in following my dreams, I wouldn't be doing it right now. Thank you.

I would also like to thank the rest of my family, who are without a doubt my biggest fans that don't read the books. Thanks guys.

I suppose I should thank a couple friends as well. I'll start with my guy Jesse, who is currently my only writer friend, because he is one of the few people who I can bounce ideas off of and trust his opinions on what does and doesn't work. Then, I'll thank Martin A.K.A. "Poopies", for assisting in the creation of the musical playlist I needed for the development of this book. A big part of my writing process is a personal playlist I make that fits the aesthetic of the project. It is how I put myself back in the creative mindset I need to be in to write, and Poopies was my go-to guy for finding the outdated rock music I needed.

I also need to thank my editor, Danielle from Hack and Slash Editing, who is doing great work at supporting independent horror authors. She has allowed my script to become the absolute best that it can be and has done so much more for me than any other editor I've ever paid. I seriously cannot thank her enough. If anyone is looking for an editor, I highly suggest you go find her.

Lastly, I would like to thank all of the readers, regardless of whether or not they liked the book. One way or another, you found it and thought something about it was intriguing enough to give it a try, and I think that's pretty cool. I've been living in this book's world for a little over a year now, and I'm just glad that other people finally get to join me there. Hopefully you liked your time dedicated to it, but if not, there's always the next one. Thank you.

Afterword

This story first came to be with a small idea around a year and a half ago—the concept for a character that eventually became Jordan. At the time, I was brainstorming for *It Came from the Loch*, and I had this idea for a hyper-meta character similar to Randy Meeks from *Scream;* but rather than following those slasher movie rules and using them to survive, they would intentionally break them, pretending to be helpless to lure out the killer and trap them. I realized later that this was essentially the opening hook to *Jason Goes to Hell: The Final Friday*, but I wanted to take this concept and make an entire story off of it.

Obviously, this character wouldn't have worked well for *It Came From the Loch*, so I tucked the thought away until a story came to mind where I could incorporate them, and eventually this one came around. Naturally, as this story developed, that character changed and became who Jordan is now. I thought that changing her into someone who was just obsessed with slasher films would make her a great suspect/mislead character, and that's just kind of what happened. I'm not really sure where I'm going with this, but I always think it's just interesting how an idea so small can evolve into something as large as this.

This book will always hold a special place in my heart, because it is my first attempt at a full-length novel with a completely original antagonist, original setting, and months of outlining prior to writing. I've always considered my first three books, the *It Came From Anthology*, to be my works of practice; and while I still feel I've got a long way to go, this book is the first that I feel to be a complete and honest representation of my work. Hopefully you enjoyed reading it as much as I enjoyed writing it.

Similar to post-credit scenes in films, I believe my readers deserve some sort of reward for making it this far past the end of the book, so I here's a small announcement: *Summer Camp for Slasher Victims* is just the first part in a trilogy. More info will come as the series comes along, but all I can give you now is the small teaser for part two:

Dust off your vintage attire and travel back in time for one night—
where every moment is sure to be a flashback!

Max's CD Tracklist

1. *Bark at the Moon* – Ozzy Osbourne

2. *Poison* – Alice Cooper

3. *South Of Heaven* – Slayer

4. *Alison Hell* – Annihilator

5. *No One Like You* – Scorpions

6. *Cold as Ice* – Foreigner

7. *Call Me* – Blondie

8. *Where Did You Sleep Last Night* – Nirvana

9. *Waiting for a Girl like You* – Foreigner

10. *Tainted Love* – Soft Cell

11. *The Four Horsemen* – Metallica

12. *Hell is Living Without You* – Alice Cooper

About the Author

Matthew Mercer is a published author and aspiring filmmaker who resides in the California Bay Area with his wife and two dogs. He is currently studying film with goals of becoming a screenwriter and director, capable of converting his horror novels into movies.

Find more from him on:

https://aspectsentertainment.com/

Facebook and Instagram: @AspectsEntertainment

Tiktok and X: @AspectsEnt

Also by Matthew Mercer

The "It Came From" Anthology

Beginning with his first book, "It Came From Above", author Matthew Mercer has taken monsters from myths and urban legends that we all know and love and placed them in stories reminiscent of 80s slasher flicks. What was initially used as a tool to learn all aspects of storytelling has become so much more; an interconnected universe with lovable characters, enticing plots, tragic happenings, and horrifying creatures. While each book is loosely connected, each one features a separate cast of characters with a unique story that can be read in any order. They are intended to be thrilling, scary, cheesy, and entertaining, so if you're looking for an equally terrifying and enjoyable time, pick one up if you dare.

It Came From Above

Mysterious disappearances. A helpless group of friends.
Will any of them survive?
Sean finally has an opportunity to take his long time crush
Samantha on a date. They go to the drive-in movie theater,
they're flirting back and forth, and everything is going
perfectly. That is, until she disappears.
In this story, reminiscent of classic 80's slasher films, Sean
and his friends try their best at finding out what really
happened that night, while trying to avoid meeting their
own demise along the way.

It Came From the Woods

What was supposed to be a simple college assignment has turned into a week-long camping trip, filmed and documented by eight friends. Their target? Bigfoot.
The footage they captured on their trip has been a matter of heavy debate for almost forty years now. In an effort to move on with her life, Nancy Miller is inviting a filmmaking crew to her home, where they will interview her while she watches her own complete and unedited copies of the footage for the very first time. Watching the people she leaves get slaughtered in the woods and reliving her greatest nightmare will be one of the worst experiences she will ever have, but getting the world to believe that Bigfoot killed your friends is not an easy task.

It Came From the Loch

Her family died on the loch, now it's her job to study it.
Decades after a tragic accident left Elizabeth an orphan,
she is making her return with her friends and daughter.
Will she find the answers she has been looking for her
whole life, or will history repeat itself?

www.ingramcontent.com/pod-product-compliance
Lightning Source LLC
Chambersburg PA
CBHW022026310726
48972CB00006B/1830